To Be Frank

Philippa Hawley

First Published in 2022 by Blossom Spring
Publishing
To Be Frank Copyright © 2022 Philippa Hawley
ISBN 978-1-7397357-2-2
E: admin@blossomspringpublishing.com
W: www.blossomspringpublishing.com
Published in the United Kingdom.

CHAPTER 1

Frank didn't get much post. He stared at the official looking white envelope, addressed to Mr Frank Roberts, 61A, Docklands Road, Felixstowe, which lay on the hall table amongst a scattered heap of flyers and adverts for pizza outlets. Next to it was something that looked like a bill for Carlos, the other lodger who lived on the top floor of Mrs West's cold, damp house. Frank hadn't received a single personal letter since Reg had become too ill to write. He picked up his envelope and took it to the kitchen, where he put the kettle on. As he made a mug of tea, Frank glanced at the envelope on the stained kitchen worktop.

While waiting for the tea to cool, he bit at his lower lip and slowly tore open the envelope to remove the letter. His hands started to shudder when he realised it was from a solicitor. *Shit*, he thought, *what have I done wrong?* The only letters he'd had from the legal profession were years ago and contained bad news.

'Dear oh dear,' he said under his breath as he read the content fully. 'Bloody hell, poor old Reg, he's gone.'

Reg Hall's funeral was to be held next Friday at the village church in Eastland. As well as announcing the arrangements, Miss Frances Freeman, the solicitor, asked Frank to make an appointment to come to see her as she had some information of interest for him.

Could just be a scam, Frank thought as he

folded the letter, tucked it in to the breast pocket of his chequered pyjama top, then took it out again and spread it on the counter to re-read as he drank his tea. He needed time to settle his thoughts, not often venturing as far as Ipswich. Eastland was even further away and Frank wondered whether he should call the solicitor's number to investigate, rather than waste bus trips. He heard the front door slam and presuming it was Carlos on his way out, decided there might just be time for a quick shower before changing for work. He'd phone the solicitor later.

It took Frank three days to make that call to Miss Freeman's office; he didn't like using the phone.

On the Friday of the funeral, Frank lurked in the churchyard of St Mary's and rolled a fag with trembling hands. He dragged on his rollie, badly in need of a smoke after the bus journey from Felixstowe to Ipswich, which felt much longer than the timetabled forty minutes. The next bus on the rural route from Ipswich to Eastland had seemed even slower, so he'd kept checking his watch, hoping he'd get there in good time.

Frank looked for a comfortable tree to lean against and at the foot of the chosen oak, he balanced his small holdall on the splayed roots, avoiding the damp January soil. He stood and watched the mourners arrive; they looked like a mixture of villagers and old friends. Even with his patchy recall, one or two seemed familiar from the past as they walked silently along the tree-lined path and into the small, stone church.

He shivered and checked his phone, ten minutes until kick-off. His plan was to slip inside after the coffin's arrival and sit quietly at the back. He'd wait until the family were settled in their seats, then he could watch from afar without them seeing him.

A small group of women bustled in at the last minute. Frank definitely recognised a couple of them from his occasional visits to Reg at the nursing home. One was still in her Arbour Gardens uniform. *Must have come straight from work, nice they'd bothered to come*, he thought. Arbour Gardens wasn't a bad place to die if your time was up. Frank felt sorry he'd not been there for a while. He stubbed out his fag and not for the first time, checked the letter was safe in his pocket. He wasn't good with paperwork but he guessed he'd need it for the solicitor's appointment the next day. The secretary had said to bring some identification, so he'd tucked a payslip into the torn envelope.

The rector appeared at the doorway and two long, black, funeral cars pulled up, completely blocking the narrow village street running through Eastland. Hardly a problem, Frank realised, as most of the villagers would already be inside, preparing to pay their last respects. The coffin tipped sideways as the undertaker's team lifted it onto their shoulders and it rocked precariously as they carried it into the church. Frank was tempted to step forward to help, after all he'd spent his working life lifting heavy weights and his shoulders were broad but still wanting to be invisible, he held back and watched the six pallbearers struggle to balance the simple pine coffin. He wondered why Reg hadn't deserved mahogany.

The rector greeted three people who stepped out of the second car. *So that's what poor old Reg's wife, Della, looked like now, not aging badly*, Frank noted. *And that's the son, Gus, all grown up and with his wife Sandra.*

The carers at the home had once shown Frank some photographs in Reg's room. The names of family members were written on the back for when Reg couldn't remember them. The nurses knew Frank wasn't close family; he'd simply told them how he and Reg had once been work-mates and that seemed to satisfy them; there was no need to say more. They simply seemed pleased Reg had a visitor.

That summer twenty years ago when Frank worked with Reg, Gus had been away at horticultural college so Frank had hardly crossed paths with the young Gus Hall. Gus looked thinner in those earlier pictures. *He's a robust fella now*, Frank thought, with a wry smile.

Looks as if he likes his beer as much as I once did, and a bit of whiskey, no doubt. Still, the lad's done well with that wife, she's a bit of a looker and a good deal younger than him, by all appearances.

As planned, Frank managed to creep inside while the organ was still playing the entrance music and he tucked his holdall under the pew in front. Frank hadn't been inside a proper parish church for years. He'd visited the chapel at the rehab centre once or twice but only went for the music; he enjoyed the reverberating tone of the chapel organ and even joined in to sing the hymns. He'd sung to Reg once when he visited and his voice had calmed the old man's agitation.

Now, as the organist started the first hymn, Frank remembered how he and Reg enjoyed listening to all kinds of music when they worked in the gardens and greenhouses of Trelawney Manor in Eastland that summer. The radio was always on when they drove round the Suffolk lanes in Reg's Land Rover and they'd talked and got to know each other.

Once the service got under way, Frank kept his eye on the congregation and noted how few hankies were in use. Across the aisle, a little in front of him, he spotted an attractive woman wearing a long, black coat and a smart hat, beneath which red curls were trying to escape. As he watched her slip off her sunglasses, he thought they were an odd accessory for January. *Maybe she was one of the few actually crying, or maybe she was just shy, hiding beneath that wide brim.* He found her most intriguing - couldn't keep his eyes off her.

He wondered how all these people fitted in with the Hall family. It made him wonder about his own family, or lack of family more like. He didn't even bear his true family name; he was Frank Roberts and always had been, getting

5

his name from the family who first fostered him as a baby. No one kept him for long, even Reg only employed him as a casual worker for one summer.

The realisation that few people in the world, let alone here in Eastland, knew or cared who he was, made Frank feel awkward and surprisingly sad. He usually tried not to ponder such thoughts but now an invisible hand seemed to grip his throat and he could hardly join in to sing the hymns during the service. A voice in his head said, *Bloody fool.*

Frank Roberts didn't usually do emotion, he'd switched that off years ago, decided it was the only way to get through life. He shuffled in his seat and accidentally kicked his holdall beneath the pew so the toiletries inside clanged against each other. He grunted 'sorry' to a plump woman in front who'd turned round and tutted. The woman with red hair turned too but she smiled and he awkwardly smiled back.

The first reading was done by a family friend called Max, who recited a poem about clocks and the passing of time. Then Oliver Trelawney read from the bible, in an important, public school sort of voice. *So that's Oliver,* thought Frank, *the son from Trelawney Manor,* away travelling when he worked there. Frank checked the Order of Service sheet on his pew and saw that the wake was to be held at the Treehouse Café in the grounds of the manor house. He wondered how different the house and gardens would be now.

After the prayers came Gus's eulogy. This

CHAPTER 4

While Frank and Mirabelle were eating their fish and chips in Ipswich, the Treehouse Café in Eastland village was buzzing with memories and catch-up conversations. Reg's widow, Della, sat quietly at a table and watched the guests exchange stories and news. Not many seemed to be thinking about Reg now he was gone, in fact most of them were talking about themselves. *I guess it'll be my turn next*, Della thought, *or maybe Maureen will beat me to it.*

Della's young friend Jenny came to join her at her table.

'How are you coping?' Jenny asked.

'I'm okay, just taking a breather. I think I've eaten too many canapés and they've given me wind,' Della replied, trying not to burp.

'It went well. I mean, there was a good turn out and the service was nice,' Jenny said.

'It's a relief it's all over. Max read the poem beautifully.'

'Thanks, I'll tell him,' Jenny said, proud of her husband.

'I'm glad Gus kept the eulogy simple,' Della sighed. 'You know I didn't want Reg to go on as he was. A diminished life like he had at the end served no purpose. At least he is at peace. I haven't even cried properly yet.'

'There's plenty of time for that,' Jenny said. 'Tears will come when you're ready.'

Della squeezed Jenny's hand.

'I was just thinking about my poor sister-in-law, I think Maureen'll feel it more than me.

She's a lonely soul and is bound to be full of guilt about missing the funeral. She hasn't been able to visit since she had her operation and that was before Christmas.'

'Hip replacement, wasn't it?' Jenny asked.

'Yes, she's really not got over it but then all her other joints are riddled with the arthritis these days. I plan to drive over to see her after the weekend and tell her about the funeral, maybe see if I can help out.'

'I didn't think you were that close,' Jenny commented.

'I guess all those years ago, we got off to a bad start. We were always very different people. She was six years younger than Reg, and just five years older than me, so sort of in between the two of us.'

'Interesting, I thought Maureen was much older than you, the way you talk about her.'

'She always seemed older, behaved as if she was Reg's guardian after their mother died. When Reg and I got together she thought I didn't love him as I should and perhaps at first that was true but we grew to be a good, steady couple.'

'And Maureen never married?' Jenny queried.

Della didn't need much of a nudge to chat on, or as Gus would say, gossip.

'Maureen wasn't keen on men in general but she adored Reg and she was good with kids - it's a shame she didn't have any herself. She trained as a librarian and loved the children who came to the library. She was a Brown Owl with the Brownies for a while too but at weekends she'd be on her own, walking in the countryside, wearing out her hips and knees. It's a good job she didn't marry - she was a hopeless cook. I bet she never got her Brownie badge for cookery.'

Della saw Jenny smirk at her harsh assessment of her one and only sister-in-law, but she didn't care, she was in her element, rattling on to a captive audience.

'Reg told me Maureen had her heart broken by her first love and never dared look at a man again. Do you know she's never cooked a roast dinner and never owned her own car? Odd woman, she took up watercolours when her joints started to go. As I say, we were very different.'

'I'm sure she'll appreciate your visit,' Jenny said looking round the room. 'Sandra has made this place really special, hasn't she?'

'Yes, indeed. I think she spends most of her time next door in the main restaurant but she still keeps an eye on the café here. She's a good woman, good for my Gus,' Della volunteered.

'Yes, they're quite a couple.'

'They both seem so focussed on work. I wish they'd slow down and start a family. I'd love to be a grandma before I'm too ancient,' Della said.

'You're still pretty fit, you'll be wonderful when the time comes,' Jenny said. 'Meanwhile, you can enjoy being a surrogate grandma to Oliver's twins. And you know you're like a third grandmother to our two scamps too, don't you?'

'That's sweet of you to say, dear.' Della straightened her specs and patted her permed hair where grey tinges were just appearing round the edges of her light brown tinted waves. 'How are they, and more to the point, where are they?' she asked.

'They're fine. They're at a friend's house for tea. We've got to pick them up shortly, so I'd better go and find Max.'

'Off you go, dear and give Jacob and little Mabel a hug from me,' Della replied.

The older woman peered over the top of her glasses. The crowd was thinning as visitors drifted away. Most came to Della's table to say sorry and thank her on the way out and between these brief encounters she watched Jenny walk between the remaining guests to find Max. He and Gus seemed to be deep in conversation. My boy looks good in his funeral suit, Della thought and she stood up to stretch her legs and go to join them. As she approached, she listened in to their conversation.

'You two look as thick as thieves,' Jenny said putting her arm round Max's waist. 'We need to go and get the kids soon.'

Max checked his watch and stood his ground. 'Gus is just telling me about Reg's will.'

'Yes, I have a copy but when I phoned the solicitor, she said she wanted to see me about an issue that's cropped up,' Gus said.

'That's odd,' Jenny said.

'I know. It looked quite straightforward to me,' Gus said. 'I was just telling Max, it's split nicely between Mum, Aunty Maureen and me. Anyway, Miss Freeman, our noble solicitor, wants me to go to the office tomorrow morning.'

Della realised she hadn't got round to reading the letter waiting for her on the sideboard at home. *It'll be nothing Gus can't deal with,* she thought, and carried on listening.

'On a Saturday?' Jenny commented.

'Miss Freeman works Saturday mornings,' Gus said.

'She does indeed, 'Max said. 'We had some dealings with her a few years ago, didn't we darling?' Max turned to Jenny.

'Let's just say we know her quite well.'

Della saw a frown spread over Jenny's face and remembered how Miss Freeman had helped them when Jacob was taken ill as a baby. It had been such a worrying time, involving their troublesome childminder and Della recalled allegations of negligence. Somehow that dreadful woman, Tricia, had got away with it by claiming mental health issues.

'Miss Freeman has a fine reputation. She's senior partner now that Dad's old solicitor's retired,' Gus said. 'I remember how she and old Mr Smith helped us trace your nanny-from-hell whose name I can hardly speak out loud, when she went off the radar. Blimey, that was a bad year.'

Jenny groaned and Della almost felt the need to butt in, but she decided not to get involved. She pretended to be busy adjusting a nearby table arrangement.

'We try not to think about our annus horribilis,' Max said. 'I'm glad you didn't mention any of that stuff in the eulogy.'

'I'm not entirely stupid. Anyway, why should I? We've all moved on. I gather that Tricia is doing okay now up north,' Gus said.

'Ha, you said her name,' Jenny said, clearly trying to sound blasé about it. 'Well, I'm pleased for Celine's sake. It must have been awful to have such a disruptive little sister.'

'Disruptive! That's not the word I'd have used,' Gus grimaced.

'At least Celine stays in contact with her now,' Jenny said. 'I'm just glad she didn't move away with her sister.'

'Yes, long may Celine stay around here so she can continue to babysit our two little terrors,' Max grinned at Jenny.

'And more importantly, help Oliver with our gorgeous god-children,' Jenny added.

'Fair comment,' Max agreed.

'And she's the only other constant in the twins' lives since their mum died,' Jenny continued.

'Family life is so important for kids. It's funny how funerals make you look back... analyse your own family life. I just can't forget how Tricia manipulated Dad in his old age,' Gus said.

Della trembled. It was time to intercede.

'Oh, listen to you lot rambling on. I thought we weren't going to talk about Tricia at this funeral. I can tell you've all been on the sparkling wine while I've stuck to mineral water,' she smiled. 'The fizz has certainly loosened your tongues. Max looks as if he's the only sober one here.'

'Designated driver,' Max announced. 'Anyway, time to change the subject, here's Oliver.'

'Gus, I need to talk to you about the will once we've helped Sandra with the clearing up,' Della said, taking Gus's arm.

'You're not doing the clearing up, Mum. I'll get you a chair and you can watch. I'll help Sandra soon. I expect Celine will be in and out of the kitchen too.'

'Anyone need a top up?' Oliver said raising the bottle of wine he was carrying.

'No thanks,' Jenny said. 'We're off in a minute.'

'None for me, either. Doctor says it affects my blood pressure tablets,' Della said.

'I will,' Gus said. 'I think I'm allowed it today of all days.

'Since when did you need an excuse?' Max teased. 'Went well, didn't it Oliver?'

'Yes, a good send-off. Gus, do tell Sandra the canapés were great. Grand, weren't they, Della? Unusual selection of guests, though,' Oliver added.

'What do you mean?' Della asked. 'It was exactly who you'd expect, family, village folk and estate workers.'

'What, so none of you saw the strange man lurking at the back, the tallish chap wearing an old donkey jacket?' Oliver continued.

'They don't call them donkey jackets these days,' Max remarked but was ignored.

They all murmured they hadn't seen anyone strange but Oliver didn't let it go. 'And there was a woman the image of Tricia there too. You must have spotted her, the one in a smart black tailored coat and a big hat? I saw red hair peeping out as I followed the coffin out and it gave me quite a jolt. She had her head down but for a minute I seriously thought it was her. I guess it can't have been though, because she didn't stop to talk and then by the time the burial was over, she'd disappeared.'

'Celine would have told us if Tricia was coming down,' Della said.

'Yes, of course,' Oliver said.

'But how would Tricia even know about the funeral unless Celine told her?' Gus said crossly. 'I'll go and find Celine.'

'Leave it, Gus. It probably wasn't even Tricia.' Della was impatient. 'It might have been someone representing the Memory Clinic or the Parkinson's team. We're dividing the collection between the charities.'

'I bet Tricia stalks us all on social media and still gets the East Anglian Daily Times posted to Manchester so she can keep an eye on us all,' Gus said.

'Sounding a bit paranoid, old boy,' Oliver clapped him on the shoulder.

'And do you wonder? This was the woman

who played havoc on your estate, caused Jacob's health problems and tried to blame my father for much of her mischief,' Gus huffed and puffed. 'Need I remind you she nearly ruined my relationship with Sandra?'

'Stop it, Gus,' Della said firmly.

'She's in a new relationship now and I hear she's had treatment and counselling. We need to hope she's in a better place,' Max said.

Della thought how anxious Jenny looked. She was very fond of Jenny, who was now gently tapping her watch, while Max was still listening to Gus.

'Let's hope her better place remains in Manchester and she doesn't bother us down here again, thank you,' Gus barked, before storming off ostensibly to find Celine.

Bloody men, Della thought.

CHAPTER 5

Frank made his way along the busy Monday morning pavements of Ipswich and started to feel nervous. He'd so enjoyed the extended stay at Mirabelle's place, that he'd almost let go of the anxiety about meeting the solicitor. Miss Freeman's call to delay the meeting for two days had worked in his favour at first, but now what?

Mirabelle didn't like him smoking in the house so he took the opportunity to roll a quick fag to steady his nerves. He wasn't used to officialdom or paperwork and wondered how he'd cope. He felt untidy in his threadbare jacket and workman-like boots, even though Mirabelle had tried to brush and perk them up for him. He threw his fag end in the gutter outside the office and took a deep breath whilst reading the sign above the door. "Smith, Smith and Freeman Solicitors". He stepped inside.

'Can I help you, sir?' asked the receptionist.

He hesitated, no-one ever called him sir.

Hold it together, Frank.

'I have an appointment ... with Miss Freeman at er... ten.'

'I'll let her know you're here. Please take a seat in the waiting area.'

Gus was already there on the far side of the waiting room, dressed in a waxed jacket and corduroy trousers, looking quite the country gent. He was exchanging a prolonged handshake with a chap in an expensive looking track suit. They both turned as Frank walked in and Frank realised the man in sportswear being greeted so warmly was Max, the poetry reader from Friday's funeral. I know you two but you don't know me yet, Frank thought and just telling himself that made him feel a bit more confident. He nodded to them across the room then sat down and hid behind a copy of the Daily Mail while he listened.

'What are you doing here?' Gus asked Max.

'I might ask you the same thing. I thought you were coming in on Saturday morning,' Max replied.

'Miss Freeman had to rearrange our meeting, some sort of mix up. Mum would have come with me on Saturday but couldn't manage it today. She's gone up to Maureen's for a few days. I said I'd be fine on my own. I think this is just a formality, I doubt we'll be here long.'

'No, Frances doesn't usually mess about. I've just been delivering some papers to her, Powers of Attorney for our parents,' Max said.

'Nice! Frances, now, is it? She's still Miss Freeman to me,' Gus sniggered. 'Why don't you hang around and we can get a coffee after?'

'That'd be good. I'm working from home today but I'm in no rush,' Max replied.

The two men sat opposite Frank and chatted quietly, discussing the funeral and their respective families. They didn't even glance across at Frank.

'Hey, you might be able to come in with me, you're so much better at these formal situations than I am,' Gus said to Max, just as

Miss Freeman emerged from her office.

'Mr Hall, would you like to come in now?' she greeted Gus and then her gaze shifted across to Frank. She seemed about to say more but Gus interrupted.

'Mum can't make it today after all, so I wonder if Max could join me, as an extra pair of ears. I think you know Max Brown,' he said.

'Well, yes, if that's what you want, it's fine by me. It might actually be helpful to have a friend with you.' She paused and nodded at Frank. 'Mr Roberts, will you please join us.'

Gus looked puzzled but stepped into the office, with Max not far behind. Frank felt unsure whether it was okay to take his overnight bag in with him. Mirabelle had given him a bit of advice about what to expect but he was still way out of his comfort zone.

'In you come,' Frances said, as if she could read his mind. 'Pop your bag in the corner.'

She straightened her smart grey suit and slipped behind another young woman already seated at one side of the desk. It took a while for the three men to settle. There was confusion about who was to sit where. Frank thought he must look rough next to the other two men, as he deposited his bag and sat down.

'We are all here in connection with the Last Will and Testament of Mr Reginald Hall. Let me do the introductions. I am Frances Freeman and this is my assistant Miss Carpenter, who will take notes. Mr Gus Hall is Reginald's son, Max Brown is Mr Hall's friend, here at his request and I'll explain the position of Mr Frank Roberts shortly but before we go any further, I did ask each of you to bring some ID. I'm going to ask Miss Carpenter to take photocopies for our records, if you agree.'

'Fine,' Gus said sharply then stared across at Frank who nodded in agreement. 'Then I wish you would explain who the heck this is and what he's doing here?'

'Thank you, Miss Carpenter,' Miss Freeman said as they passed their documents across the desk. 'All in good time, Mr Hall. Can I call you Gus? Now, as I said when I phoned you on Saturday morning, I can't apologise enough for having to rearrange this appointment. I'm so sorry your mother can't join us but she has indicated she's happy for us to proceed without her. I'm sure it's only right she's with her sister-in-law at this sad time.' Miss Freeman took a breath and then smiled at Frank. 'Mr Roberts, Frank, thank you so much for agreeing to stay in town a little longer. As you know, we will cover the cost of your accommodation for the extra days.'

Gus looked at Max, raised his eyebrows and shrugged his shoulders.

'That's very good of you love, I mean, Miss Freeman. My boss has changed my shifts around so everything's under control.'

'Good, then let's make a start,' she said tapping the documents on her desk. 'Gus, I need to inform you that the 1990 Will you and your mother have in your possession is not in fact Reginald Hall's final Will and Testament.

He had a more recent one drawn up by my retired colleague, Mr Smith, in 2010 and that is the document I have here.'

Gus looked surprised. 'I didn't know. Shouldn't we have been informed?'

'That was up to your father. He obviously kept it to himself and that was his right.'

'I don't like the sound of this,' Gus muttered to Max with a puzzled expression.

'I've had copies made for you and your mother, Gus, as well as one for Maureen and Frank.' She passed the new papers across the table. Each had an envelope clipped to them. 'Your father recognised that the contents of the new will were a little unusual so he wrote a private letter to each of you in turn, as well as including a simple explanation within the document itself. The letters, as you can see, are sealed.'

'I'm getting worried now. Please can we get to the crunch?' Gus said.

Frank took his cheap ready-readers from an inside pocket, put them on carefully and peered at his letter, realising Gus's expectations were greater than his own. He noticed sweat gathering on Gus's ruddy face and wished he had a clean handkerchief to offer. Gus's solution was to wipe the sleeve of his shirt across his brow.

'It's quite a complex will but in summary, Reginald Hall wishes his final estate, after probate to be divided as follows... it's easier if I read it, "To Miss Maureen Hall, my sister, I leave the sum of £10,000 with which to provide

'I can take it from here. Thanks for your help but I really should phone his mum and get him home.'

CHAPTER 7

Frank felt uncomfortable as he dawdled towards the bus station. He wasn't sure if it was the will or Reg's letter that had rattled him, or more likely the poor little boy vomiting on his boots. He was worried he shouldn't have taken the boy's coat off. If the woman wasn't so agitated, she might have challenged him in public. Frank knew damn well he presented no risk to the kid but you had to be so careful these days. He hadn't got much out of the boy when he talked to him in the gents' toilet, it wasn't as if he had much experience with children, but that little chap seemed anxious and not just because he'd been sick. The boy was twitchy, wouldn't even tell him his name and remained on the verge of tears, even after a good wash.

Something here's not right.

Jacob Brown, he thought, *that name on his coat makes sense.* Frank remembered Gus asking Max about his children in the waiting area outside Miss Freeman's office. He was sure he called them Jacob and Martha. No Mabel! That was it, Jacob and Mabel, what funny old-fashioned names. *Poor kids*, he'd thought at the time.

And the more he thought about it, Frank was certain the woman Jacob called Tricia was someone he'd seen twice before. He remembered a woman of similar build, leaving the nursing home as he arrived one time, her red hair half hidden by a dark scarf.

Something about Tricia had struck a chord at the funeral and he was starting to work out why. It was the same woman. On each occasion she looked like an imposter. He knew how that felt, he'd felt like an imposter all his life, especially this morning at the solicitors.

Max seemed a good man though, helping poor Gus, who'd looked as if his heart had been pulverised. It was a good job he'd had his mate with him. Frank wondered if Gus was still there at the solicitors, getting information about how to contest a will. He found his mobile and rang Miss Freeman's office to check but the receptionist wouldn't give any information away.

It wasn't until Frank insisted that there might be potential harm to a child and his call was urgent, that the receptionist eventually put him through. Frank asked Miss Freeman to confirm Max's surname was Brown and then explained why he was worried. After hearing the crux of the story Miss Freeman went into gear and asked for the details of the café. She said she'd phone Max and give him Frank's number and also ask Miss Carpenter to call the police to see if any missing children have been reported.

Frank picked up the call from Max at the first ring on the phone and swiftly explained that he'd seen a boy he thought was called Jacob Brown at the café and the boy had seemed upset.

'Oh my God, where are you now?' Max shouted.

'At the bus station. I saw a woman called Tricia leave the café with the boy and I think they were heading for the car park.'

'Why didn't you stop them? Which car park?'

'The one near the bus station. It's only when I phoned Miss Freeman and told her my concerns, I thought it might be your son.'

'Go to the car park and I'll join you there. I'm at the library and it's bloody chaos. Jacob's little friend and her mother are in tears and making no sense. No one knows how Jacob managed to disappear. The librarians are dashing about, searching for him and are about to call the police.'

'Hold on, just get yourself over to the bus station car park and be quick. Meanwhile I'll try to keep them here,' Frank said.

Frank arrived at the car park, hoping it was the right one and that Tricia hadn't parked in the multi-storey further down the road. At least this near one was on one level but he hadn't a clue what he'd actually do when he got there. He'd have to think of something. He smoothed his untidy hair, straightened his jacket and guessed he'd be able to invent some sort of stalling tactic when the moment came. Surely Max wouldn't be far behind him.

The car park was only three-quarters full and at the far end he spotted the little green Mini. The passenger door was open and Tricia was bending over doing up Jacob's seat belt. He looked around. *Shit, there was no barrier at the exit and no attendant to ask for help.*

Up to you then Frankie boy.

He walked up to the car trying to look casual.

'Hi there! Excuse me for bothering you but I've been thinking since I left, I should have asked for your number.'

Tricia slammed shut the passenger door and walked round to the driver's side.

'I don't think so,' she said curtly and jumped into the car.

Frank put his leg out to stop her closing her door and tried not to react to the pain that ran through his trapped left thigh.

'Can we go home now?' Jacob whined.

'It's all right, Jacob,' Frank said to the boy, then looked again at Tricia. Without her bobble hat on, she really did have amazing hair. 'Look, I'm new in town and to be honest, a bit lonely. I'd love to meet up with you later, after you've dropped the boy off, that is,' Frank said in his calmest voice, trying to maintain the smile of a charmer, despite the throbbing of his thigh.

'I'm not local, just visiting, so we'll leave it at that. I need to shut the door now.'

'Don't be like that,' Frank said. 'I'd really like to get to know you better.'

'I said no, so piss off,' Tricia hissed, as if she meant it but was still trying not to alarm Jacob.

Frank reached in and snatched the keys from the ignition and slammed the door shut. He leaned hard against it. He was wondering if he should limp round to the passenger side to try to get the boy out, when Gus arrived to solve the dilemma.

'Max called me,' Gus told Frank. 'He's on his way.'

Tricia was now screeching in the driver's seat and trying to open the door. Much to Frank's relief, Gus extricated the confused little boy and then pressed himself against the passenger door so they must have looked like bookends.

'Uncle Gus, what are you doing here? She was going to take me home,' Jacob said.

Gus held him in a bear hug and said, 'don't you worry, Daddy's on his way. There's been a bit of a mix up.'

Gus twisted to look at Frank, while Tricia banged on the window inside.

'We'd better keep her where she is for now,' Gus called across the roof of the car.

Teamwork, eh!

Frank looked around and saw Max running across the car park to join them. Max grabbed Jacob from Gus, making Frank feel surprisingly moved by such a reunion, until Jacob shrieked, 'Dad, you're squashing me!'

'I'll squash you if I want to. I might never let you go, even if you do smell of vomit,' Max laughed, releasing his grip and pretending to hold his nose.

'What do we do now?' Frank asked.

'Call the police and tell them where we are,' Max said. 'Frances has already warned them something's happening. We should phone her too because she'll be worried.'

'I'll call Miss Freeman while Gus informs the fuzz,' Frank said. 'You look after your boy,

Sgt Goffey appeared, as if on cue. 'Miss Patricia Bird, you can leave now,' he said. 'You are to go to your sister's home, in her care, and she will supervise your usual medication. We've taken the advice of your psychiatrist in Manchester, who knows you well and has spoken to our doctor on the phone. Please don't let the doctors or your sister down. Do not leave the area, do not fly away, Miss Bird,' he smirked. 'We need to see you back here tomorrow afternoon. Can you agree to that?'

'Yes, thank you,' said Tricia sounding unusually biddable.

'We've moved your car to the police pound overnight and it'll be released to you tomorrow if you can make arrangements. Any longer than 24 hours and you'll be charged a fee,' Sgt Goffey said.

'I can collect it,' James offered.

'And we'll need you, Patricia...'

'Tricia,' she announced.

'Tricia,' Sgt Goffey continued, unabashed, 'we'll need you to report in each afternoon after that, until we've processed the other statements and got the full, written psychiatric report from Manchester. Only then will you know the outcome of this,' he smiled.

'That bugger's enjoying keeping me on tenterhooks,' Tricia murmured on the way to Celine's car.

CHAPTER 9

'No, Gus, I've heard enough. Put the phone down, I'm coming straight home.'

'Mum, listen, I don't want you driving in the dark. I'll come to you first thing in the morning. I need to see Maureen too.'

'I can talk to Maureen, you've told me all I need to know,' Della replied.

'There's a bit more, actually and I have letters for both of you.'

'More? Whatever else can there be? I knew what the will said.'

'Mum, you're not listening, there was another will, a more recent one. The one you have no longer stands.'

'It'll be fine, Mr Smith did it.'

'No, it won't be fine, it's been rewritten and I'm trying to tell you we aren't getting much. Dad's left nearly everything to a man we don't even know.'

'Well, your dad didn't have much, so it won't make that much difference and I knew he'd want to give something to his sister. It must be a mix up about a stranger getting anything,' she said.

'Oh Mum, never mind the details now, I'll bring you a copy in the morning and we'll go over it together. I'll set off straight after breakfast.'

'Okay. I need to speak to Jenny now and check Jacob is okay.'

'That can wait, Mum. Jacob's home, safe and sound and no doubt tucked up in bed by

'This Frank chap told us he was fostered, adoption never went ahead,' Gus persisted despite his aunt's emotion. 'Said he was brought up in children's homes but thinks you might be his mum.'

Della shook her head and looked at her sister-in-law in disbelief.

'I don't know if we can believe him,' Gus said. 'Do you have a copy of your baby's birth certificate, Aunty Maureen? And what about the father? We could check with him. If not, I think we need some genetic testing done before we accept any of this.'

'The father never met the baby. We weren't together by then. I don't remember being given a birth certificate. Maybe Mum had took it, but I don't recall. They took my baby away very suddenly when he was only a few weeks old and I was in such a state they could have given us a letter from the Queen and I wouldn't have noticed.'

'No father,' Della sighed.

Maureen searched in the sleeve of her cardigan for a new, fresh hanky.

'That's why we need genetic testing then,' Gus persisted. 'Would you be up for that?'

'I haven't much choice,' Maureen sobbed. 'I've turned him away enough times, I can't do it again.'

'Again?' Della questioned.

'He tried to phone and I put the phone down.'

'He said he wrote too,' Gus said.

'I tore the letters up.' Maureen stifled

another sob, struggled to her feet and steadying herself on the furniture, she limped from the room.

'Oh, Gus, you're right, this is awful, so much worse than I expected,' Della said.

'Let's give her a moment. I haven't told you the full story about Jacob's escapades either. He didn't just get lost - he was taken.'

'Taken! Who by?'

'You'll never believe it, but Tricia kidnapped him. Sorry, but there was too much to tell you in one phone call last night.'

'Lord save us! Go on then, tell me, while Maureen gathers herself,' Della sighed. 'I'll make more coffee first and find some biscuits, blow to my indigestion, I need sugar.'

Over more coffee, Gus recounted the tale he'd managed to assemble about the storytelling session at the library with Jacob's best friend, Lola, and her mum and how Jacob apparently refused to use the ladies when Janet, the friend's mother, took Lola in. He went to the gents on his own and when he came out, Lola and Janet were nowhere to be seen. Tricia was lurking nearby and she took him away.

'Slow down, Gus, I can't keep up. What sort of mother lets a six-year-old go to the gents on his own in a strange place?'

'I know, it's ridiculous. Jenny and Max will have had words with Janet about that,' Gus agreed.

'And surely, Jacob must know not to go off

CHAPTER 10

Frank was grateful for a quiet night in the warehouse. He couldn't believe how tired the past four chaotic days had made him. When he got home to his dingy lodgings in Docklands Road after his shift, he couldn't sleep. He hated working nights and was never great at sleeping in the daytime but today was worse than ever. His bed felt cold and hard after the cosy bed at Mirabelle's and his thoughts kept jolting in different directions. He tossed and turned and dozed on and off for most of the morning but when the cleaner started vacuuming the stairs, he gave up and went down to make tea and toast.

'Morning,' grunted the cleaner. 'Sorry, did I wake you?'

'No worries. Couldn't sleep. I'm putting the kettle on for a cuppa before I shower. One for you?'

'No, ta, I'm not staying long today. I'll nip up and quickly do the bathroom before you use it.'

'I shouldn't bother, I'll only mess it up again. Why not take an early?'

'Wouldn't mind, just don't tell Mrs West.'

'As if I would.' He forced a smile and before he knew it, she had her coat on and was out of the door.

Frank munched his toast and took the mug of tea back upstairs. He bent to retrieve a cardboard box from beneath his bed and felt his back twinge. *Yes, definitely getting too old for this*, he thought, even though his duties were lighter, now he was working in one of the smaller warehouses. Sitting on the threadbare armchair next to the bed, he leaned forward and tipped the contents of the box out. He immediately regretted sending the cleaner home as fluffy clumps of dust fell from the lid and between the papers. There were a couple of folders, some loose documents and a few brown envelopes to work through. Various letters, many of which were water stained, were folded in tatty plastic bags.

What a mess. Long overdue for a sort out.

A few of the brown envelopes were from HMRC about tax and he was relieved to be able to prove that he was a real person with an identity. His address, NI number and a date of birth were clearly visible, so he put the most relevant pieces on one side to take to Frances Freeman. She wanted a utility bill too, but the best he could offer was an O2 mobile phone contract. He rearranged a reasonably clean folder in which to store anything else that might be considered important and then kept on looking.

He unearthed a couple of birthday cards from Irene, the most long-standing girlfriend he'd ever had and that was before his final time in rehab. She was a boozer too, so he had to leave her behind when he divorced himself from alcohol. He wondered what she's up to now. *Hopefully she's not dead.* He realised he hadn't had a lover, a woman friend, or even much of a social life for the past twenty years. A photo of him and Reg in Arbour Gardens turned up next. It was tucked into a pamphlet about the residential home, with one almost illegible letter from Reg. He chucked the leaflet in the bin, put the letter in the folder, then propped up the picture up on the single, dusty chest of drawers where he kept most of his clothes. The wood of the wardrobe standing next to it was annoyingly lighter in colour and he gave it a little kick as he went back to his paperwork.

Frank ignored the other faded old letters about random appointments at the Alcohol Advisory Service and the Magistrates' Court and wondered why the heck he'd bothered to keep them. When he got down to the grey folder from Social Services, his breathing quickened and he felt his chest tighten and his back twinge again.

You fool, you've seen it all before, you only need to check there's nothing useful there to show the solicitor.

Frank spent so much time alone, he didn't exactly talk out loud to himself but often had conversations inside his head. It worried him that recently he was doing it more often and the voice was sounding more real. When he'd mentioned it to Mirabelle at the weekend, she suggested he keep a journal to write down his thoughts instead of holding them in his head. She'd offered him a spare notebook, the cover of which had a picture of a ginger cat on it and that had made him smile. Mirabelle said if you wrote things down, especially important things and worries, it was like putting them in storage and you could let them go without losing them forever. He liked that idea. He got up, stretched his legs and reached for his holdall, where he found the cat notebook. With a biro from his top drawer, he wrote his name, address and date of birth in the front page and then congratulated himself for making a start. His breathing settled. Even with that small beginning, he felt able to open the folder.

In the grey folder, he read through that old stuff, mostly written in faded ink on flimsy yellowing paper, the smudged ink showing signs of water damage. No birth certificate turned up. He rifled over and over though the dusty papers. Another statement he thought he'd once seen - about his discharge from social care when he reached eighteen - was also missing. He wished he'd cared more, been more organised with his personal documents and generally looked after himself better, instead of drinking himself silly. If he had a better filing system, he might not have lost so much information in the house flood. He went ahead and jotted in his new notebook odd words and phrases he could decipher from his early records that seemed important – "No physical abnormalities", "Feeds well", "9 month milestones satisfactory", "Settling". This was all good, why and when did it all seem to change?

The next set of dates were poorly written in smudged ink as if the papers had simply been caught in the rain, and some were torn. Worrying words appeared in different handwriting – "Night Terrors", "Episode of

reflected a strange, ghostly light in the front windows. When she got out of the car, she saw condensation creeping down inside the glass, thin streams of water making patterns inside.

'Odd,' she muttered, as she opened the front door and felt the damp chill. She checked the hall radiator and it felt steely cold, even though she was sure she'd left the heating on. She flicked on the lights and went to check the boiler. A green sign was flashing ERROR. She put her bags down and keeping her coat on, searched for the instruction manual. She tried to reset the pilot light and ignite the burner. The boiler made a whooshing sound but failed to light and the flashing continued.

She walked through the bungalow and found no other problems, apart from cold radiators and zero hot water. She closed the curtains in the sitting room and both bedrooms and toyed with the idea of using her electric convector heater to get her though the night but in the end gave in and phoned Gus.

'I'll come and get you, Mum, you can spend the night with us and we'll phone the gas people first thing in the morning,' he said.

She knew he'd say that - he didn't even seem cross, bless him. A net curtain of guilt about ruining their evening settled over her as she waited and she thought of Maureen, relatively immobile and alone in Lowestoft. *She'd never had a son she could call on in an emergency. It's no wonder the old girl sometimes got a bit crabby.*

Chestnut Cottage was warm and cosy and Sandra had prepared a generous lasagne, enough for three. *Fish and chips could wait for another night*, Della thought. She unpacked her bag in the spare room and joined them at the table.

'There's some salad to go with this,' Sandra said. 'Here's the vinaigrette.'

'I'd rather have some mayonnaise, if you have some, or else salad cream will do,' Della said.

'Mum! 'Gus said. 'You never change, do you?'

'Should I?' she asked.

'Course not, you have whatever you want,' Sandra said. 'Gus is a bit grumpy at the moment, I'm sure you can guess why.'

Soon they were on to the will, going round in circles, talking over the same things they'd discussed at Maureen's.

'We can manage,' Sandra said. 'You're going to have to let it go, Gus.'

'How many times do I have to say it, it's not about the money, it's the rejection and having to think why?'

'I realise I'm paying for the past, so don't worry about me, but I'm sure you've done nothing to cause his silly decision,' Della snapped. 'That Frank really must have got under his skin. I'm cross with myself that I didn't realise he was still in Reg's life. It's years since he left the area.'

'I'm seeing the solicitor again next week to consider contesting the will and we'll try to get

Frank's genetic testing sorted out.'

'That's going to cost,' Sandra said.

'You're the one who says we can manage,' Gus snapped.

'Hey, don't take it out on me.' Sandra got up to clear the table.

'Steady on, you two,' Della said. 'Go and relax and I'll do the washing up. I've been sitting around too much and need to get moving. Find me an apron while I put the rest of this salad in the fridge.'

Della opened the fridge door and bent to clear a space on a low shelf.

'What are all these boxes?' she enquired. 'There's no space left in here.'

'Oh, they're nothing important. I'll have a sort out tomorrow,' Sandra said. She quickly pushed the door shut and grabbed the salad bowl. 'The salad can go in the big fridge in the utility room for now.'

Sandra stayed and dried the dishes while Della washed.

'He'll settle down,' Sandra said. 'He's just got a lot on at the moment.'

'And how about you dear? Are you alright?'

'I will be,' Sandra said, but Della thought she didn't sound convinced.

Della excused herself and went to her room for an early night, saying she'd not slept well in Lowestoft. She heard Gus and Sandra muttering in the front room until late. *So much for a good night's sleep*, Della thought, *The sooner I can get back to my own bed the better. Bloody Reg - he's caused all this unsettled behaviour. I'd like to give him a good talking to.*

She didn't know if she was dreaming or half-awake and thinking. Memories of Reg and Arthur, Oliver being widowed and Celine helping him look after his motherless twins, drifted through her mind. The old days on the Trelawney estate still seemed real but then she jerked and was fully awake.

Once the boiler's fixed I must go and see Celine, Della thought. *I need to check Jacob and the Browns too. People need fixing as well as boilers, I should make a list. I wonder what's in those boxes in the fridge?* was her final thought before she dozed off again.

CHAPTER 12

Della kept out of the way and let Gus go to supervise the boiler repair, giving her time to catch up with her phone calls. Celine, usually so warm and welcoming, sounded distracted when Della asked if she could pop over for a cuppa.

'It's not very convenient this week, maybe next week,' Celine replied.

'Oh dear, are you on duty at Drift House this week?' Della enquired. 'It's not half-term yet surely? I could come early before the school pick up?'

'It's not that. We have visitors.'

'I see. Someone interesting?' Della asked bluntly.

'Not exactly, Tricia's here and James has come down to help. They have to stay here until the police sort things out.'

'Of course, Gus told me all about her taking Jacob. I didn't realise she was still there. I'm so sorry.'

'It's a bit complicated, the police want her to stay in the area while they tie up some lose ends.'

'Poor you, no wonder you don't want me there. How's your wife coping with it?'

'As you know Lynn finds Tricia very difficult. She just goes off to work and leaves me to it, and James goes out walking Alfie instead of staying with Tricia. The dog's loving it of course, all those extra, long walks. I wish Tricia would go with them but I think she's avoiding him.'

'Trouble in paradise?'

'Wait a moment, I'd better go into the garden to talk... Yes, they had a huge row about her coming to the funeral and she said he gave her a black eye, which he of course denies. I didn't know what think.'

'Is he aggressive, then?' Della said.

'No, he always seems very measured, as you'd expect from a trained psychologist. I feel bad, Tricia didn't really want me to drag him down from Manchester. Perhaps I shouldn't have. Maybe they need more space?'

'You must have had good reason,' Della replied.

'I panicked.'

'That's not like you?' Della said.

'I thought he'd help me, give her a character reference, explain this was simply a blip. After all, he was her counsellor before they became a couple. He should know better than anyone how to handle her when she has one of her wild spells.'

'She once told me he'd been her salvation, so maybe he will again and she can go back up north,' Della said.

'I do hope so. I'd actually stopped worrying about her but this week I've had have trouble even getting away to do the afternoon school run. When I do, I have to leave James in charge, which is tricky.'

'What, in case she skips bail?'

'She's not exactly on bail, they're calling it tying things up. James seems to think she'll

'Excellent.'

'Sorry, I'm going on about our lot but your family have more than a few problems too. Let me make us a sandwich for lunch and you must tell me all your woes.'

'Just a piece of fruit for me thanks, I'm not eating bread at the moment. Losing some weight might help my indigestion. Now where shall I start?' Della said.

'How about working back from the busted boiler,' Jenny said. 'It'll put my worries into perspective.'

Frank had three days off after his night duties before starting back on days. As always, it took him that long to get his sleep pattern back on track and his mind straight again. He was feeling restless now and had time to make some appointments. He needed to book a haircut, make a long overdue dental appointment and also check the date for the next meeting of the community choir. He'd seen a poster for the choir in the cafeteria at work and liking the line "no experience necessary", had jotted down the time and place on a scrap of paper. As he rummaged around in his bedside cabinet to find it, he hummed a hymn from the funeral.

Frank knew he was putting off the most important thing, which was making an appointment with Miss Freeman to deliver his extra documents. He was stalling, building up courage for the genetic testing. He couldn't blame Gus for wanting it - in a way he wanted it too - but he was scared. What if Maureen wasn't his real mum after all? He couldn't stand it if the bubble of hope for a better future was burst by a simple blood test or mouth swab.

Jesus, you don't even know how they do it or how long it takes.

When he eventually called Miss Freeman's office and made the appointment, a mild sense of achievement settled over him and with the date safely in his cat book, not owning a diary

The next morning Frank found Mirabelle in the kitchen, beating batter in a bowl.

'Pancakes?' she asked. 'Pour your own tea.'

'Yes please, to both that is.'

'Good, I'm running in a pancake race next week and I need some practice,' Mirabelle announced.

'We don't have to go for a run now, do we?' Frank asked with some alarm.

'No, you chump. To be fair I'll probably walk, maybe trot. I'm not built for running but my priority is to do a good toss so let's get to it. Stand back, here comes the first.'

The large, soft pudding of a pancake slopped onto the floor.

'I think you've made it too thick.' Frank said stifling a snort.

'I agree.' Mirabelle added a glug of milk. 'Your turn now.'

Frank melted some butter and poured the loosened mixture into the hot non-stick pan. He shook it back and forth, just as he'd seen the TV chefs do. The pancake slid about pleasingly.

'Here we go,' he said.

The pancake flew into the air, nudged the overhead lampshade and dangled momentarily, leaving Frank and Mirabelle in breathless suspense. It finally dropped down and Frank caught it as a crumpled mass in the pan. They both bent over with laughter.

'So,' spluttered Mirabelle having caught her breath, 'we've got the batter right and the pan works, now it's all down to the flicks and tosses. Let's go for an edible one next.'

The next two or three came out well and they sat and ate them with a squeeze of lemon and a sprinkling of sugar.

'That was grand,' Frank said, as he wiped his mouth on a nice clean napkin. 'When's the race?'

'Tuesday afternoon.'

'I wish I could stay to watch,' Frank said. 'Any chance of some pictures?'

'I'll ask my friend, Apricot, she only volunteers part-time at the library so should be free.'

'Apricot? What is it with the fruity names?' Frank asked.

'Her real name's Avril but she doesn't like it. Her hair is sort of apricot coloured.'

'Fair enough,' Frank said. 'Is it Ipswich Library? I mentioned the hoo-hah there with Jacob on the phone, didn't I? I wonder if Apricot knows about it?'

'Yes, we've spoken about it. They've taken it very seriously at the library, had an internal investigation and put extra safeguarding training in place. I gather they're going to employ a security guard. Hey, you could apply for the job.'

'I don't think that would work,' Frank said. He looked down at the table and considered whether now was the time to point out his police record, pathetically minor though it was. He decided the answer was no, not when things were going so well. She knew about the children's homes and his alcoholic past and that was enough for now.

'I haven't got the right background or training. I'd probably be too old anyway.'

'Perhaps,' she said.

'But I'm glad they've taken action. That'll please Jacob's parents. By the way, someone left a book in my room.'

'Yes, I did. I thought you might like it. Apricot often passes on books to me or I buy them second-hand, that's why I have so many on the shelves. They do an excellent second-hand book sale for charity every now and then at the library too.'

'Sounds counterproductive.'

'It's to bring the community into the building, you know, encourage people who wouldn't otherwise use a library. That's why they do events like the storytelling, to make it more child friendly. Sometimes they host art exhibitions, it's all about making libraries more sustainable.'

'It's child friendly so long as a child doesn't get lost,' Frank blurted out.

'Yes, quite, but that's being addressed, isn't it? Let's stay positive, Frank. I do like to stay positive you know,' Mirabelle said firmly and Frank felt he was being reprimanded like a child.

He gave her a lop-sided smile, conciliatory with a tinge of cheekiness.

Mirabelle continued, 'On a more positive note, I'm exhibiting some of my pictures at the library this summer. I thought you might like to come for another visit?'

'I'd be most honoured,' he replied. 'Can I borrow the book and bring it back when I return?'

'Of course you can, and take a couple more with you too, in case you don't come back too soon.'

'Is that a dig?' He felt brave enough to tease her back. 'I'm quite a slow reader, but I'd like to read more. Trouble is, I never know what to look for on a bookshelf. I could do with some recommendations.'

Mirabelle led him into the front room and they surveyed the shelves. Frank declined "Moby Dick" for being too long and "The DaVinci Code" for looking too complicated. He settled on "The Curious Incident of the Dog in the Night-Time" and a poetry collection by Spike Milligan.

'Great choices,' Mirabelle agreed and Frank hoped she was being supportive and not condescending. He just prayed he was up to this new world he was entering.

'How's the journal writing going?' Mirabelle asked when they went back into the kitchen.

'On and off,' he replied, without admitting he used it more as a diary than a journal. 'Hey, I'll help with the washing up and then I thought we could go for a walk, I'm not seeing the solicitor until after lunch. I could treat you to a meal out if we're quick about it.'

'Don't worry, we're not made of money. Let's come back home and have sandwiches.'

Mirabelle and Frank put on their coats and boots and set off for the waterfront. Mirabelle's

CHAPTER 14

'So, there's no birth certificate, and compelling though these other reports and papers are, I think we now need the genetic evidence,' Miss Freeman said.

'I was prepared for that,' Frank agreed. 'Let's get it over and done with."

He rolled up his sleeve.

'Oh, it'll be a mouth swab and we don't do it here,' Miss Freeman laughed. 'We have an arrangement with a private clinic in the town. I'll give you a referral. They cost a little more but you get a better service than the online agencies provide. This place includes counselling before and after if needed.'

'Okay, I see. How much? I've not got a lot of spare,' Frank told her.

Miss Freeman pushed a leaflet across her desk.

'Jesus!' gasped Frank.

'I know it looks a lot but they'll have to swab Maureen too of course. It's taken some discussion on the phone to her solicitor but she's agreed to go ahead if you do. I had a feeling it would come to this so forgive me for already paving the way. We can take the payment out of the estate account. Any questions? Do you need time to think it over?'

Frank went quiet. He wished Mirabelle was with him to hold his hand and give her advice. Her mind was so much sharper than his and she would know if this was the right way to go. Miss Freeman shuffled the papers on her desk and took a sip of water.

'I agree,' Frank finally said.

'Good, I'm sure that's a good decision,' she said. 'I've taken the liberty of making you a provisional appointment at the clinic for later this afternoon. Would you like me to confirm it while you're here, it'll save you travelling back and forth from Felixstowe?'

'Might as well go for it,' Frank said, his heart thumping at the thought.

'I'll arrange for them to send the bill to me so all you need to do is fill in a form and let them do a mouth swab. The results take a few days to come back.'

'Mouth swab, that's good. How will I get the results?'

'They'll send a hard copy so you have the written evidence. It makes it easier to process the results emotionally if read it in your own time. An emotionally charged phone call can be difficult to absorb.'

'Fair enough,' Frank said thoughtfully.

'As Maureen is almost housebound, Gus is going up tomorrow to do her sample.'

'Is he qualified? What if he cheats? He could take a swab from a complete stranger,' Frank said.

'Mr Thomas, that's Maureen's solicitor in Lowestoft, will meet him there and witness it,' Miss Freeman replied. 'I assure you it'll all be done correctly.'

'That's going to add to the costs. Can't Gus drive her down here?'

'I did suggest that but Maureen, I mean Ms

Hall, wouldn't agree. To be honest, it's taken a lot of persuasion to get her to accept a swab at all so I think this is the best we can do.'

Frank checked his watch as he left. He just had time to call in at Bangers and Burgers for a late lunch. He ordered a cup of tea and a slice of toast from a waitress and rang Mirabelle's number to tell her he'd be late back.

There was no answer. He thought she must have done more window-shopping or called in on a friend. He found his reading glasses and slowly tapped out a text with his clumsy fingers.

"Having swab test this afternoon, hope to be back about 4.30. Frank."

He altered it before pressing send, worried she might think he was at the sexual health clinic. He'd not been there for a while!

"Having genetic test swab this afternoon, hope to be back about 4.30. Frank."

He picked up a discarded local newspaper from the empty table next to him and after reading the headlines, went to the jobs vacant page. The security job at the library was listed and one or two other things that might fit the bill. He quietly tore out the page and tucked it in his pocket.

He paid his bill and made his way to the clinic. He imagined he'd probably be less nervous if he was heading for the sexual health clinic. The end of this short walk would potentially be a major turning point.

The clinic staff were charming. He saw on

the notice board that there were a number of private rooms with different practitioners working – a private osteopath, a nutritionist and reflexologist, a counsellor and a travel jabs doctor. Frank had no idea such places existed. He didn't even have a GP, just went to the walk-in-centre if he needed medical advice.

The genetic screening took place in an upstairs room. An assistant explained the plan and helped him fill in the complex form. When he didn't know all the answers she said, 'Don't worry, that's why we're here. Just fill in what you can. Doctor Mikael will see you shortly, he'll do the rest and take the swab. Do you have any more questions?'

As he waited to be called, Frank checked his phone for texts. Nothing. That's odd, he thought but before he could send another message to Mirabelle, he was called into the doctor's room.

Frank walked to Mirabelle's house thinking it was all much easier than expected. He imagined waiting for the results would be the hard part. The clinic warned him not to have unrealistic expectations and he wondered if that was their way of saying they didn't believe him. He'd had days when he didn't believe it himself, he just wished he could remain as positive as Mirabelle. He was a lucky man to have met such a remarkable woman, he thought. What a coincidence that her parents had done some fostering when she was a girl. He guessed that's how she got to be so understanding.

He rounded the corner of her road and saw the house was still in darkness. He let himself in with the spare key and turned on the hall light. He looked around to see if she'd left him a note. There was no sign of her coat on the hook, no discarded Doc Martins on the mat.

'Mirabelle,' he called. 'Where are you hiding?'

It would be just like her to jump out and surprise him.

'Mirabelle,' he called again, only louder.

He checked the downstairs rooms then went upstairs. He opened the bathroom door carefully in case she'd collapsed or was on the loo and was relieved that neither was the case. All three bedrooms were empty. He checked his phone and there was still no reply to his text. He called her mobile once more and this time it was answered by a male voice.

'Mrs Jones' phone. Who's calling?'

'Frank Roberts, who's that?' he replied.

There was a muffled pause.

'I'm her friend,' Frank continued.' Can I speak to her, who are you?'

'I'm a nurse at the A and E department. She's nodding so I'll hand you over to her now. She's going to be fine.'

'Mirabelle, what's happened? Are you alright?'

'Hi Frank. I'm fine. I tripped on a kerb and landed on the sharp edge of a metal drain. I've had a tetanus jab and they're just stitching me up.'

'For goodness' sake! Nothing broken I hope?' Frank asked.

'No, I had an X-ray. My leg's really swollen with the bruising though.'

'You poor thing, I'll be right over, what's the address?'

'Thanks.' Mirabelle gave him the address then said, 'I think we might need a taxi to get me home Frank, so leave it half and hour. Call a taxi and when you get here ask the driver to wait outside. They say I shouldn't walk on it for a few days.'

When Frank arrived, he saw Mirabelle's leg had been dressed. One side of her blooded, brocade dungarees was rolled up to her knee and the bandaged leg was resting on a stool. Two nurses had to help Frank transfer her to a wheelchair in what must have looked like a scene from a farce.

'Phew! I'm glad I shaved my legs and it's a good job the trousers of these are baggy,' she laughed as Frank wheeled her to the waiting taxi. 'I wouldn't have wanted that nice male nurse to see me in my knickers.'

'Or me?' Frank chuckled, wondering if her legs had been shaved in his honour.

'Sorry, love, don't speak too soon, I might need you to help me out of these clothes when we get home. I've wrenched my shoulder too so I might be a bit useless for a while.'

Frank couldn't think of a suitable reply other than to smile and hoped he didn't look too awkward.

Back at the house, Frank put the kettle on for a cup of tea, then following Mirabelle's instructions, he went upstairs and found her an easy-to-put-on kaftan and a warm dressing gown. After some help undoing the buckles, she managed to wriggle out of the top half of the dungarees with a reasonable degree of decorum. Frank was pleased to see she kept on the loose T-shirt that covered her top half. The bottom half was more of a challenge. Frank draped the dressing gown over Mirabelle's lap and carefully tried to lower the bottom of the baggy outfit while Mirabelle raised her hips. The fabric of the injured leg had been cut vertically by the nurses before being rolled up to gain access to the wound but the material of other leg was stiff with blood and surprisingly resistant.

'Just go for it, Frank,' she declared. 'Give it a good pull and never mind if it rips some more, the outfit's ruined anyway. Ouch! Mind the shin.'

'Sorry. Wow, this bandage is bigger than I realised. How long's the flipping cut?' he asked, once her leg was fully exposed.

'Four or five inches, and because of its position and all the bruising, they've put a pressure bandage on. The district nurse is coming in the day after tomorrow. I'm to keep it elevated until then.'

'It's quite serious, then. You'd better do as you're told. I'll be in charge for the time being,' he pulled an exasperated face. 'I've got some overdue holiday I can take but I'll have to go back to work by the end of the week.'

Mirabelle chuckled. 'I know, don't worry, I'm sure Apricot will help if necessary. I'll call her tomorrow but thanks Frank, you're a good chap. Now what shall we eat? Tell me what's your speciality, beans on toast or scrambled eggs?'

'Beans might be safest. Tomorrow you can give me an armchair cookery lesson,' he replied. 'Now are you warm enough?'

'I think so but maybe I need a sip of brandy for delayed shock,' she said with a grin.

'Any excuse,' he said. 'I won't join you, if you don't mind.'

CHAPTER 15

The text on Della's phone that morning was simple and direct.

"She's gone. Coffee 11.00. Usual place. C x"

"Perfect. Dx"

"See you then. C x"

"Looking forward to it. Dx"

Della went to change from her everyday, around-the-house clothes into something tidier. She decided cleaning the kitchen floor following the boiler repair would wait until later. How they'd made so much mess was beyond her but at least she was home again and the bungalow was warm. She made a list of shopping to pick up on the way back from the coffee date.

Della found Celine sitting at their favourite table with two cups and a large cafetière of coffee perched in front of her. On each saucer sat a small biscotti biscuit and Della briefly frowned. She preferred the cellophane wrapped gingery biscuits that were kinder to her teeth. She'd just have to dip.

'Sorry I'm a bit late,' she said, 'couldn't find a parking space.'

Della sat down and Celine pushed the plunger slowly through the hot liquid.

'I'm always terrified these things will explode on me,' Celine said. 'You look nice, new coat? You're not spending Reg's money already, are you?'

'You must be joking, don't tell me you haven't heard,' Della said. 'I thought everyone would know by now.'

'Know what? I'm out of the loop, I've been supervising Tricia for the best part of a week.'

'Oh yes, so she's gone but where to? Hospital, custody or home?'

'Home. Thankfully Max decided not to press charges. The police have issued a police information notice and Tricia had to sign it to say she won't make uninvited contact with Jacob or harass his family.'

'Can they do that without charging her?' Della asked.

'It seems so. Anyway, Tricia and James are back on track and he's taking responsibility for her.'

'Responsibility?'

'Yes, making sure she continues with counselling, medication and psychiatric reviews.'

'So, they don't think she'll do it again, I mean take another child?'

'No, it wasn't as bad as it first seemed. She swore she simply wanted to spend some time with Jacob and things got out of hand. They don't think she's a risk to the general public and she has to learn to address her obsession with Jacob through counselling. The notice means if she makes contact with Jacob again, she'll be in trouble. I do hope this has finally taught her a lesson,' Celine sighed.

'She's like a cat with nine lives, that one,' Della commented. 'Is James up to the task?'

'I think so. He's a good fellow and he loves her. Everything settled once she calmed down.

I'm going to phone them for regular updates and go up to visit more often.'

'With Lynn?'

'Probably best on my own,' Celine screwed up her face. 'I put my head in the sand when Tricia moved up to Manchester but I realise I need to step up and be a more supportive sister.'

'That's very admirable. I hope Lynn agrees.'

'She's fine, just doesn't want to get personally involved.'

'What do you think it is that makes Tricia as she is? She's so unlike you. Once she left the area, I was busy looking after Reg and I never really asked you. Perhaps I didn't really want to know,' Della said.

'I've given it a lot of thought. I'm tempted to say too many sunbeds frazzled her brain but in reality, it goes back to childhood and our wayward mum. You know we had different fathers?

'Yes, I knew that much.'

'My dad was steady and he brought me up when his marriage to Mum ended. She went from man to man, fell pregnant on a one-night stand, had Tricia and in the end raised her on her own with lots of transient uncles.'

'Not a great role model then?' Della said.

'No. Tricia developed the same propensity for men. She never found the right one, despite always wanting a family of her own.'

'And that never happened.'

'She only recently let on to me that she'd had several miscarriages along the way.'

123

'I knew she was quite a bit younger than you and you'd not been in touch much. It's a sad story,' Della sighed.

'I thought I was doing the right thing letting her come to stay at Trelawney Manor when she remade contact and was out of work. I can't help feel guilty for letting her into our Suffolk lives.'

'You weren't to know how it would turn out, Celine.' Della reached across the table and patted her friend's hand.

'She had good references as a child-minder,' Celine said.

'Yes, that's what Jenny told me.' Della nodded. 'And it's hardly your fault my Gus chose to have an affair with her, distracting her from her duties.'

'Oh, I can't bear to think about it.' Celine found a tissue to blow her nose.

'It's a good thing she moved away and met James, isn't it?' Della tried to lighten the tone of the conversation which had got much deeper than she'd expected.

Celine smiled. 'I thought James had helped her find some acceptance at last but hearing about the funeral then revisiting Eastland, seeing Gus, Max and Oliver, must have triggered something in her.'

'I think we need more coffee,' Della suggested and waved at the waitress.

'Yes, now enough of me, we should be talking about you and your problems.'

Celine blew her nose again and sat back to listen while Della explained all about the will and Reg's money and how Frank Roberts was getting most of it. Celine listened with her mouth hanging open.

'What *the* Frank Roberts, the hero who found Jacob? That's astonishing. I couldn't work out how he fitted in, thought he was just a passing Good Samaritan,' Celine said.

'It's more than that. He reckons he's Maureen's illegitimate son. That makes him Reg's nephew... and he's a recovering alcoholic!'

'Jeepers, and Gus's cousin,' Celine said. 'It's like a soap opera.'

'We're just waiting for the DNA results.'

'DNA results, flipping heck, I can't believe it, poor you,' Celine shook her head. 'Poor Gus, and Sandra too. They could really do with the cash to help pay for their treatment.'

Della's eyebrows puckered behind her gold-rimmed glasses.

'Have I just put my foot in it?' Celine asked. 'You probably don't want to talk about that.'

'What treatment?'

'The er...'

'Spit it out.'

'The IVF. I thought you knew. Oh God, I'm so sorry.'

'That makes sense. I found some boxes in the fridge the other day. Sandra was so odd about it I thought they were up to no good and were hiding stolen goods, or drugs or something.'

'What? You thought those two were stealing truffles or caviar from the restaurant –

hilarious!' Celine started to laugh and soon Della was giggling too. Once they started, they couldn't stop. They tittered and snorted. Heads were turned in the coffee shop and the other customers smiled along with the two women, even though they'd no idea what the joke was.

The waitress came to the table. 'You ladies having a good time?'

'Yes. Please can we have more coffee, dear?' Della said, 'and we'll have two chocolate brownies as well please.'

'So long as they're not laced with anything illegal,' Celine teased when the young waitress had gone and that set them off laughing again.

'You've no idea how much good this is doing me,' Della said eventually. I haven't laughed like this in ages. I was miserable at the funeral and then staying at Maureen's didn't help. Coming home to a broken boiler just about topped it.'

'I don't laugh enough either these days, not now I see the twins so much less,' Celine said.

'They're growing up, that's for sure.'

'Yes, and Drift House is a good twenty-minute drive from my place. It was so much easier when I could just walk to the manor to get to them. Now I only see them on days I do the school run and then I just stay for an hour or so until Charlotte gets home from work.'

'How are you getting on with the step-mother?' Della asked, emphasising the word step-mother.

'Fine, she's okay. The girls seem fond of her too but she's not like their real mum.'

bit on the money of course.'

'What sort of obstacles?' Mirabelle asked.

'Now's as good a time to tell you as ever,' Frank sighed.

'What you mean now you've seen me in my undies?' she said.

'Ha, maybe,' Frank cleared his throat. 'Before we get in any deeper, I need you to know I have a criminal record – it's in the past, of course, but it could affect my work prospects.'

'Okay...' Mirabelle hesitated. 'Tell me all.'

Frank told her more about his days as an alcoholic and his cannabis laden past. He told her about his appearances in the Magistrate's Courts of North London and South Essex, but swore since he'd been sober in Suffolk, and kept a clean slate. He'd never actually been detained in prison.

'That's not too awful Frank, everyone has a past. The right job will come along, mind you I like the phrase sober in Suffolk. I'm not daft, you told me you once had a drink problem and I spotted from the off you always opted for cola or alcohol-free lager.'

'You still trust me, then?' he asked.

'I do. Don't look so sheepish. You're doing alright and none of this is the end of the world.' Mirabelle readjusted her pillows and rubbed her shoulder.

'Not the end of us, you mean?' Frank dared a smile.

'It's early days but we're good together. I'd like to let things run for a while. How about you?'

'Same,' Frank replied. 'Better get you to the bathroom now. Then I'll do the washing up. Shout if you need me.'

'Rubber gloves are in the cupboard under the sink.'

'These hands don't need gloves,' he quipped. 'I'm tough, remember?'

It was late on in the morning by the time Mirabelle had washed and dressed and with Frank's help, managed to get downstairs. Once she'd settled in an easy chair, cushioned stool under her leg and phone by her side, Frank set off on his shopping trip. Walking though the outskirts of Ipswich, he took in the scenery. He could see the metal towers of lights peeping from the top of the Ipswich Town football stadium in the far distance. It was ages since he'd been to a proper football match. The last one he went to at Felixstowe and Walton FC had been disappointing. Maybe Ipswich Town might be more appealing. He was tempted to walk that way to check the place out, maybe see how much tickets were or even if they had jobs in the offing, but a wave of uncertainty suddenly spread over him. He headed back towards the more familiar waterfront where he and Mirabelle had walked before. He wanted so much to stay positive but was starting to panic. There might be more potential for him here than in Felixstowe but was he asking too much? Would just having more money really change his world? He walked on, clutching the *away. It's Mirabelle's infectious excitability that's doing it. You need to slow things down. Feet on the ground. You already have a job and a place to live.*

He carried on walking and went past Bangers and Burgers and looked in to see if there were any familiar faces inside. He wondered how little Jacob was and what had happened to the crazy redhead. If he and his cousin Gus were in touch, he could ask him more about her, but the chances of that were slim. Frank carried on wandering aimlessly and soon found himself on the road near the football stadium.

Any point in asking there for a job? Probably not quite ready yet.

He kept on walking, happy to be alone and used to his own company. Beyond the stadium he followed a path beside the river and just kept putting one foot in front of the other. He didn't really know where he was but that didn't matter. Eventually he found himself at The Marina. His feet were aching but he knew the road to take.

CHAPTER 17

Apricot had done a good job styling Mirabelle's hair and after a few days of rest, Frank thought how bonny she looked. He aimed to be back home at his lodgings in Docklands Road by the time Apricot returned. Next time she said she would bring some special scissors with the promise of a trim. That woman had endless skills.

He made himself scarce when the district nurse arrived - another capable woman. He went out walking again, not being used to having all these females around him. He'd never before understood the saying about men and women being as far apart as Mars and Venus. This time when he returned, Mirabelle's leg was visibly more comfortable, the dressing had been changed and she was able to move about the house with greater ease. She even threatened to take up light kitchen duties. Thankfully, she dropped the subject of Frank's employment prospects after, in a down-beat voice, he reported on his view of the Job Centre.

Their relationship was now back to where he felt comfortable; a developing friendship with hopeful prospects of more to come. Frank liked that. He suspected that while he was out walking and thinking, Mirabelle was doing some similar soul-searching. He wondered how much of a heart-to-heart she and Apricot had shared too.

'I need to go back home soon,' he announced

at breakfast one morning. 'I'm on stand-by for a weekend shift, then working every day next week.'

'I knew you'd soon be off. Thanks for staying this long. It's been lovely, I couldn't have managed without you.'

'It's been my pleasure. Can you manage now? I guess you've always got Apricot.'

'I think I prefer you, she can be awfully bossy,' Mirabelle chuckled.

'I can see what you mean. I'll be back before long, if you'll have me?'

'Do you need to ask?'

'Perhaps not. Would you like a copy of my work rota so you know when my days off are? It'll be easier to plan the comings and goings.'

'I'd like that. You're not running away then?'

'No, but we need to take our time with this thing. It is a thing, isn't it?'

'It's a thing,' she agreed with a grin. 'There's no rush. We can talk on the phone and you're welcome here whenever. Who knows, I might even get to Felixstowe one day.'

On the bus back to his other life, Frank could smell the left-over portion of last night's vegetable lasagne that Mirabelle had made and tucked into his holdall. It was in a silver takeaway carton with a cardboard lid and wrapped in a plastic bag to avoid leakage but he was still mildly aware of the whiff of onions and garlic. It would have been embarrassing had the bus not been almost empty. At least he didn't have to go to the shops on his way home and once the lasagne had gone, he'd eat at work until he had time to restock his cupboard.

Mrs West was out and co-lodger Carlos was shut away in his room. Frank warmed the lasagne and thought it tasted even better than the night before. He found himself missing Mirabelle and feeling ridiculous for being so daft. He'd spent his life never relying on anyone else. He had thought he was ready to get back to his own place for some peace and quiet but now he was here, he was already planning his return trip.

Sure you don't just want the woman to cook and wash up for you?

'Shut up. That's not it,' Frank blurted out loud, shocking himself.

Frank's brief conversation with the voice inside his head irritated him as he washed up his plate. A court psychiatrist once asked him whether he heard voices other than his own and he said no because this voice was most definitely his own. Up until now he'd only ever heard his own voice, loud and clear, and usually just when he was troubled or stressed but recently, he'd occasionally heard Mirabelle's.

You're getting soft in your old age, letting that woman get under your skin. What are you scared of? She's kind and funny and intelligent. That's it, intelligent and bright. What does she see in you? Surely not just the money? She really doesn't seem that kind of person and you haven't got the money yet. Might never get it.

She gets lonely and doesn't want to grow old on her own. Isn't that a good enough reason? Perhaps it is, because you feel much the same.

Frank tramped upstairs to his dull little room with its single bed and one comfy chair. He looked at the picture of him and Reg perched on the top his chest of drawers and managed a smile. He persuaded himself that keeping busy back at work would soon sort him out. He might also finally make it to the community choir meeting this week.

Frank knew immediately what was in the long, white envelope that arrived in the post three days later. He picked it up from the mat with trembling fingers and returned to his room, where he propped it up on his chest of drawers where he usually put important things. He convinced himself the result wasn't due for a few more days yet still felt nervous. How dare they send it early when he was unprepared and not due to see Mirabelle for another week? Whatever it said, he didn't want to tell her by phone, he'd have to keep it to himself for seven whole days.

He took a deep breath, donned his reading glasses and opened the envelope. He had to read it three times and go over all the terms and conditions and clauses before he could absorb the contents. Eventually he accepted the result, written there in black and white. The conclusion was that with a 99.9% degree of certainty, Frank Roberts was Maureen Hall's son.

Frank flopped back on his bed and closed his eyes. His heart jumped inside his ribcage and his fingers started to tingle.

This is no time to have a heart attack Frank. Stay calm, breathe.

When he felt able to sit up, he checked his watch and saw he still had a couple of hours before the afternoon shift. He felt the racing pulse at his wrist and confirmed he was at least, still alive and therefore fit for work. He wondered if it was wise to go for the walk he'd been planning but he couldn't just sit around with all that adrenaline coursing through him. He decided a trip to the supermarket might be the answer, where he could pick up some treats for himself and maybe a magazine to take to Mirabelle next week.

He wondered if Maureen had received her letter too and whether she'd told Della and Gus yet. That family, no, *his* family would be in an even greater state of agitation than him and he wondered what they would do. When he got back from shopping, he rang Frances Freeman's secretary and booked an appointment to meet with her when he was next in Ipswich. Until then, he'd let the information settle in his mind. He hoped Maureen or Gus wouldn't phone him in the meantime, he wasn't sure what he would say and how he could cope with that just yet.

CHAPTER 18

Frank still had Mirabelle's spare key but didn't use it on his return. He rang the bell and wriggled his toes inside his boots as he waited for her to open the door. As soon as she appeared, he thrust the bag of gifts from the supermarket into her hand. A small bunch of pink roses poked out from the top and he almost squashed them as he bent forward to kiss her purple painted lips.

'What have I done to deserve all this?' she asked, once she'd regained her poise.

'Nothing, I'm just pleased to be back. You look good.' He stroked the purple streak of hair that had replaced the green one. 'This is good.'

'Apricot did it to match my lipstick.'

'So I see, very plummy,' Frank said.

She laughed coyly.

'I see the leg's much better,' he commented as he watched her hips sway down the hall.

'Yes, the stitches are out and the scar's looking good.' With a swish, she raised the hem of her blue and purple dress to show him. 'But I might never get that contract as a stocking model now. I'll put the kettle on and you can tell me what you've been up to. There's a Welsh hotpot in the oven for later.'

'Welsh hotpot?'

'Yes, Lancashire hotpot but with Welsh lamb,' she grinned.

She opened the chocolates he'd brought to have with their cups of tea and they caught up so easily that Frank wondered what he'd been worrying about. She was kind and funny and she seemed to genuinely enjoy his company. He felt happy and relaxed in this house, which was much warmer than Docklands Road in so many ways.

You're beginning to know who you are, Frank.

After dinner, they lounged on the settee holding hands and listening to a programme about Bob Dylan on the radio. Frank hummed along with the tunes and joined in with the chorus of "Mr Tambourine Man".

'You have such a nice tone to your voice when you sing. Have you made contact with that choir yet?' Mirabelle asked.

'I've phoned but they're having a half-term break.'

'Shame,' she said. 'Why the sudden frown? I promise I'm not going to nag you. I'm just interested.'

Frank took a deep breath.

'The letter's arrived,' he said.

'The letter? Oh, *the* letter and you're frowning? My giddy aunt and gobsmacked cat, how could you keep me waiting? Tell me what it said.'

'I now know that... Maureen Hall is my mother and I am her son,' Frank said boldly.

Tears filled Mirabelle's eyes and one trickled onto her cheek.

'Why are you crying?' Frank produced a clean hanky from his pocket and dabbed her face.

'It's wonderful, I'm just so happy for you but

an agreement or a compromise,' Frank suggested and Mirabelle nodded, 'but I need to make contact with Maureen first.'

'I agree you should make contact with Maureen Hall as your next step and I can help you with that. Are you happy for me to talk to her solicitor? As you know, he and I have already made contact and he seems a decent sort of chap. I would suggest you ask to visit her in Lowestoft and he could be present at the meeting.'

'I could go with you, Frank,' Mirabelle offered. 'It might help to have another woman present.'

'Of course, her sister-in-law might want to be there too,' Miss Freeman said. 'Just don't do anything rash, Frank. Leave it with me and I'll make some calls.'

They walked slowly back to the taxi rank. Frank was quiet and thoughtful about the future. Mirabelle took his arm and leaned in a little.

Suddenly he spoke. 'Mirabelle?'

She looked at him, brows furrowed.

'I wish we'd booked lunch instead an evening meal,' he said, 'I'm starving.'

'Me too. We can change it. I'll call them and we can make it a long leisurely lunch then go home and have a snooze in front of the telly.'

CHAPTER 19

Della put the phone down and sat at her dining table, waiting for the shaking to stop. She blinked and reached across for the stamp album that had been dominating her thoughts ever since Oliver and his new wife had brought it back from an initial valuation. Della still called Charlotte "the new wife", even though she and Oliver had been together for at least three years. She wasn't sure about Charlotte - whatever Celine had said, Della thought she was a bit of a know-it-all. She angrily swept the album in its well-padded cover, to the floor. She had to literally hold her leg still to prevent herself from kicking it. A lone, lilac coloured stamp escaped from one of the leaves and fluttered onto the carpet. The stony face of Queen Victoria looked up at her as if to chastise and Della immediately felt foolish. She hoped she hadn't damaged the album, even though it was a ridiculously pathetic legacy from her stupid husband.

She picked it up with a sigh of despondency but also relief that no real harm had been done, and restored Queen Victoria to her rightful place in the album. Perhaps the next valuation might be higher. Oliver did say he had someone else in mind, a specialist dealer who might be interested. She decided to phone Gus and invite him to lunch to discuss it.

Gus arrived at midday and greeted his mother with a hug.

CHAPTER 20

Miss Carpenter rang with a message from Miss Freeman while Frank was still at Mirabelle's. Gus and Della Hall were soon to make a visit to Maureen Hall for a family conference and Miss Freeman suggested Frank should wait until after that before trying to see his mother. His mother was apparently in a very unsettled state. She suggested a simple letter in the meantime might ease the way.

'What did she say?' Mirabelle asked.

Frank gathered her leg was recovering well but she still sat with it elevated in the front room whenever possible. She'd probably been able to eavesdrop most of the message.

'Thinks I should write but I'm no good at letters,' Frank groaned.

'Would you like me to help?' Mirabelle offered and Frank nodded. 'You make a pot of tea and I'll find a pen and paper. Presumably you have the address?'

'Yes, Reg gave me his sister's address ages ago when he was staying with her. Something made me keep it, fate I suppose. God, I don't even know what to call her,' Frank said.

It took several drafts to get it anywhere near right. Mirabelle read it out loud to see if it sounded okay.

"Dear Maureen Hall,
I am sorry this has been a difficult time for you and I hope you have now been able to accept the results of our recent DNA tests. I

155

am very pleased to be able to acknowledge you as my mother and hope one day you will feel the same way about me as your son. I would very much like to meet you now, in a safe place, with people you trust also present. Your sister-in-law and nephew might want to be there and I, in turn, could bring a trusted friend. If you would prefer to initially communicate by phone, please tell me.

Can I suggest we take this slowly and try to have reasonable expectations of what our future relationship might be? We do not have to even think about Reg's will until after probate is granted, so to begin with, let us just meet and try to be calm and understanding about each other's position.

With best wishes,

Frank Roberts (this is the name by which I am known)."

'It's a bit wordy. It doesn't really sound like me,' Frank said.

'Okay, how about in that second sentence, just saying I am glad to know you are my mother?' Mirabelle suggested.

'Yes, that's more me. And we could leave out the will bit altogether until we've met,' Frank said.

Mirabelle did some crossing out.

'You're right, simple is better. Are you going to handwrite this or type it on my computer?' she asked.

'I think I'll write it, that'll make it more personal,' Frank decided, after a brief pause.

'Have you got some decent writing paper?'

'I have and you can use my best Parker pen too,' she said, and gave him an encouraging smile as she went to her desk drawer. 'It was a leaving present when I finished at the council.'

Frank was annoyed with himself for making a couple of mistakes on the first draft. He even spelt Felixstowe wrong in his address but the second time round, he went more slowly and was satisfied with the result.

'I wonder if she'll reply. I feel like a schoolboy writing to a pen friend, I only had to do that once at primary school, when I had to write to a girl in Malawi. I didn't even know where Malawi was at the time.' Frank shook his head then laughed. 'To be fair, the only letters I've written since were to Reg and he didn't worry about grammar.'

'Go and put your feet up while I put supper on. How about corned beef hash?'

'Grand. Is it Welsh beef?' Frank said.

'Argentinian, I think,' she giggled.

'Have you got a map so I can see how far away Lowestoft is?'

'The road map's on the bottom bookshelf,' she called on her way into the kitchen. 'I think it's about forty miles. There are trains direct from Ipswich.'

Frank put on Radio 2 and studied the map of Suffolk. He thought it would be nicer to go by road and see the countryside but as they had no car and he couldn't drive, that was unlikely. Lowestoft looked bigger on the map than he'd expected, and not so far from

Kessingland, where he knew Bill, his work friend, took his holidays. Frank let his eyes wander round the county, imagining what all the little towns and villages must be like and recalling their odd Suffolk names. He tried but couldn't find Eastland on the map. He wondered if that was because it was too small a village to even deserve naming. It only consisted of one big house with a few workers' cottages, the church and a tiny village store.

It had only taken half an hour or so by bus from Ipswich to Reg's funeral but now it was as if the place didn't exist. He knew it must, because the bus driver on the number 23 bus from Ipswich knew exactly where Lawn House was. He said he'd once been to a wedding reception at the Lawn House garden restaurant, so could tell Frank when to get off and how to find the church.

Frank looked further afield and cast his eye towards Stowmarket to the northwest, remembering that was where Jacob lived with his family. He knew that was a fair drive from Eastland. He recognised other villages from the old days of driving around with Reg, names like Monewden and Dallinghoo. They'd laughed at the name Debach, which they always called Debauch. He knew Reg's nursing home was north of Ipswich, more in the direction of Woodbridge but he still couldn't find Eastland. He started thinking about where his new-found, extended family lived and he wished once again that he could drive a car and go and explore the area in person, not just on a map. His eyelids drooped.

He was dreaming of dinner in a posh restaurant, maybe it was at Lawn House, when Mirabelle woke him.

'I can't find it,' he muttered, half asleep.

'What love? What have you lost?' she asked.

'Eastland. I can't find it on the map.'

'I think it's just east of Monewden, yes look there, between Monewden and Easton, where that little black dot is marked with a capital E.'

'For goodness' sake, how is anyone meant to find that?' Frank snapped.

'Maybe they don't want people to find it. Perhaps they liked their privacy in that grand house you've told me about.'

'You can't have privacy and run a business, that's one of the problems with owning a gaff like that,' Frank said.

'Hark at you, all knowledgeable about the landed gentry. Come on, your dinner's ready.'

'All this thinking is wearing me out. I need an early night.'

CHAPTER 21

Frank and Mirabelle spoke to each other on the phone most evenings over the next two weeks when he was back in Felixstowe. He proudly told her he'd enjoyed his first time at the community choir and the delight in her voice made the effort he'd made worthwhile.

'Tell me all about it. What did you sing?' she asked.

'There were some weird voice exercises then we sang "Swing Low Sweet Chariot" and a few other things. It was a really nice bunch of people. More women than men, so they were pleased to have me.'

'That's wonderful, Frank. I'm so proud of you but I don't want those blue eyes of yours to go wandering.'

'No risk of that. I don't have time for another woman in my life,' he quipped. 'I've got too many women on my mind as it is.'

He told her he was worrying about not having heard back from Frances Freeman and nor had he received a reply from Maureen. At least his letter hadn't come back marked "Return to Sender". There was still hope.

'I expect she's still mulling it over,' Mirabelle said kindly.

'I don't know what to do next.' Frank was despondent.

'Have you considered reaching out to Gus?' she asked. 'Apricot and I were talking about it today and she thought that was worth a try.'

'Apricot is the expert now, is she?'

'She did handle her own divorce and she's not daft. She said sometimes you have to make more noise in order to be heard.'

'The solicitor said not to deal directly with the family so as not to rub them up the wrong way. If we remain amicable, there'll be less likelihood of them contesting.'

'Fair enough. Why don't you just phone her office, you've given her enough time?' Mirabelle said.

'I might be able to in the morning but it's not easy to make calls from work,' Frank moaned.

'You don't think you could have missed her call?' Mirabelle queried.

'I'm not completely useless,' Frank barked.

'I know you're not, sorry. You sound tired so I'll say cheerio and we'll have another word tomorrow, about sevenish when you're home. Okay?'

The next night Frank was more positive. He'd got through to Frances Freeman, who explained Maureen had been taken ill with cellulitis not long after Gus and Della's visit. Anyway, she'd had a few days in hospital for treatment and was now home and on the mend. No decisions could be made until she was well enough. Della was keen to see things progress though and she hoped that they could all to agree to meet soon. After running through Frank's work schedule, Miss Freeman pencilled in some dates to suggest.

Mirabelle had some news to share too. She and Apricot had considered transport arrangements for Lowestoft and Apricot had very kindly offered to drive them.

'I said we'd pay for petrol and treat her to lunch to say thanks,' Mirabelle told him.

'That's kind of her,' Frank said cautiously. 'But is it too much? You don't think she's getting over-involved, do you?'

'She's my friend, Frank, and she is kind. She's also a bit lonely and helping people makes her feel wanted.'

'I'm not sure she likes me,' Frank said.

'Why?'

'Just the way she looks at me.' Frank might not have dared to say that to Mirabelle's face but over the phone it was easier.

'Now you're being daft, Frank. Maybe you don't like her? Why do you always think the worst? I do wish you could have a bit more faith in yourself,' Mirabelle said.

'Me too,' Frank sighed.

'Hey, come on now, snap out of it. Things are looking up and soon you'll be meeting your mother. Are you coming to Ipswich this weekend or waiting until the week after so we can tie it in with Lowestoft?'

After a pause Frank replied, 'the week after would make more sense, if that's all right? I'll have another choir session to report on by then too.'

'It's fine, Frank. We'll talk again tomorrow, if you can fit me in,' her laugh sounded false. 'I'll have checked the dates with Apricot by then.'

'Okay. It is very kind of Apricot. Please say thank you.'

Frank put the phone down and asked

himself why he was unsure about Apricot.

It's the silly name.

He smiled at himself. Maybe Apricot foolishly thought he was stealing her best friend. She probably had never had to share Mirabelle before. Perhaps he should talk to Mirabelle about that?

Mirabelle's an odd name too, just about acceptable.

The very next day Frank got an email from Miss Freeman, on his mobile phone, saying everything was set up for a meeting in Lowestoft a week on Saturday. He wished he was at Mirabelle's with her big computer screen. He found his glasses and read that Gus and Della would be spending the whole day with Maureen and her solicitor would arrive at 2 pm sharp. She suggested Frank and his friend then arrive promptly at 2.10 pm.

Another message came in from Gus, who proposed that he and Frank should have a brief phone call that evening to double check arrangements and break the ice.

It took Frank ages to tap a couple of sentences to reply. The small screen made him prone to typos and the autocorrect facility seemed to make his spelling worse, not better. He wondered if he should send the email to Mirabelle to check, but decided that was lame and it was indeed time he had more faith in himself. Perhaps he just needed new glasses. He re-read the message twice and then as Mirabelle had encouraged him to do, he read it out loud to see if it sounded right. After pressing send with a shaking hand, he tapped Gus's phone number into his contact list, relieved that his communication skills were improving.

The feeling didn't last and that evening, when he called Gus, he was once more feeling unsure of himself.

'Hello, it's Frank here, Frank Roberts. You er... thought we should talk?' Frank faltered.

'I know who you bloody well are, Frank. Thanks for calling, how are you?'

'Okay thanks, how about you?'

'Good. Now let's cut to the chase. I want you to realise how hard this is for Maureen and I trust you'll be really gentle with her next Saturday.'

'Course I will. I just want to meet up and start to get to know her. We don't even need to speak about the will if she doesn't want to.'

'You know my mum will be there too, so be prepared, she'll certainly want to talk about it. Mum's no pushover and nor am I. We'll be watching your every move.'

'There's no need to be threatening, Cousin!' Frank emphasised the word cousin and then said what Mirabelle might say. 'Let's be kind and calm with each other. There's no need for any nastiness.'

'Easy for you, you're getting my money,' Gus said. He sounded as if he was actually spitting.

'It's not your money, it's Reg's and the decision he made was his alone. Listen to me, I'm prepared for some negotiation in due course, once we have probate, but in the meantime all I want is to meet Maureen.'

'Pah!' Gus spat again.

'And I'd like to meet you again. I seem to remember you and I worked quite well together in the car park, rescuing Jacob that afternoon. How is the little lad?' Frank asked.

'He's fine, thanks and you were a great help but it doesn't mean we have to be best friends.'

'But we can be civil. What happened to the redhead?' Frank asked.

'Tricia, she's all right. She was let off with a warning and some sort of supervision order. She's gone back to live with her boyfriend in Manchester.'

'That's good. Interesting character, eh?'

'That's one way of putting it. Perhaps I'll tell you all about her one day,' Gus said.

'If we're still speaking to each other by then?' Frank said.

'I imagine we might have to be,' Gus replied.

'It might help to find out a bit more about each other, now we're family,' Frank said. 'You never know we might find we can help each other.'

'We'll see,' Gus's voice hardened again. 'I'll see you just after two next Saturday.'

'Sure, but before you go, can you give me some directions for the house?'

'Don't you have satnav or a bloody map?' Gus snapped.

You need to watch this chap and his short fuse. You might be the one with a criminal record but he's the one who oozes aggression. Stay calm, Frank.

165

'A friend has offered to drive. I'd like to make the journey as easy as possible for her.'

Gus quickly gave some simple directions, from which Frank only managed to jot down one or two key points. He wasn't too worried, because of course Mirabelle had a map. Mirabelle liked her maps. They managed to end the call on a steadier note, which Frank thought was a step in the right direction and he was even happier later that evening when Mirabelle praised him for handling Gus so well.

Frank spent the rest of the night wondering how he should introduce Mirabelle to Maureen and the others at the meeting. Was saying 'good friend' good enough? Did 'trusted friend' sound too formal? 'Girlfriend' seemed wrong at their age and 'lady friend' sounded either old fashioned or pervy, while 'partner' was more like a long-term business arrangement. He'd have to see what Mirabelle preferred.

Good friend, maybe!

CHAPTER 22

Apricot came to collect them in an orange coloured Nissan Micra that almost clashed with her hair. It was a smart little car but looked too small for three adults. Frank hadn't thought about what sort of vehicle she owned when he'd agreed but then he was pleasantly surprised by how comfortable it was when he climbed in the back and found his long legs fitted nicely. Mirabelle sat in front with a road map spread across her lap and Apricot tapped the postcode of Maureen's house into the satnav. Once again, Frank felt redundant as he listened to the women chatter, only being interrupted from time to time by the posh, recorded male voice giving directions. Frank smoothed the new shirt he was wearing and straightened his recently dry-cleaned jacket. When he first put it on, he wondered if it had shrunk at the cleaners or had he put on weight with Mirabelle's home cooking.

Apricot was an unpredictable driver, heavy of foot when alternating between pedals. She jerked forward in fast spurts and braked far too late at junctions. Frank wished once more that he could be the driver.

One day.

He checked his seat belt was secure and tried to catch Mirabelle's eye in the wing mirror. She didn't seem to notice the jolts of her belt squashing her bosom. Even from behind Frank could see how the fabric straps pulled.

After an early lunch in Woodbridge, when Frank was actually able to join in the conversation, he began to feel more relaxed. He removed his jacket for added comfort when they got back to the car and to his delight, Mirabelle offered to take the back seat. She carefully placed his jacket next to her. Apricot directed her conversation at Frank, then as they continued up the A12, passing signposts to Debach and Easton to the left and Snape to the right, Frank felt the memories coming back when they passed near Eastland again. He made Apricot laugh by relating how he and Reg used to say Debauch instead of Debach when they passed the road sign. In return, Apricot told him how she enjoyed going to concerts at Snape and wasn't that an odd name too? It made her think of a wading bird or a snake like Plum's funny stair rail.

From behind Mirabelle chipped in, 'I've never been to Snape.'

'Do you like music, Frank? The three of us could go there to a concert one day,' Apricot suggested.

'Frank's quite musical, actually,' Mirabelle announced from the back. 'He has a fine voice. He's a member of a choir.'

'How lovely. Are you a tenor, Frank? I imagine you are,' Apricot said, knowingly.

Frank wasn't certain if he was a tenor or not, he just sang as it came out of his mouth. The choirmaster was relaxed about such things and didn't give labels. Frank decided the best thing was to agree with Apricot and call himself a tenor. He looked out of the window at the passing countryside while the women turned to the subject of Mirabelle's future art show at the library.

They drove on through Blythburgh and he saw a sign to the coast at Southwold and then Kessingland. Frank thought of Bill's holidays again and how he'd talked about a huge turbine at Lowestoft Ness, perfectly placed to catch the winds coming in from the North Sea. Frank looked at his watch, and then the satnav screen, which showed they'd be at their destination in just twenty-eight minutes. He felt his stomach grip and this time not because of Apricot's driving.

'We're going to be early,' he said.

'Better than being late,' Mirabelle said. 'Can we find somewhere to freshen up before the last stretch?'

'We'll get round the ring road first, then I'll look for somewhere,' Apricot replied.

'Gus said we should aim towards the Ness and then turn off down the Yarmouth Road. The road we're heading for is towards the seafront. There might be somewhere at the Ness for a breather and I could see the giant turbine I've heard about,' Frank said.

'There not time for much of a stop, but I'm sure we'll get a bit of a view of that on the way,' Apricot announced.

They negotiated the busy ring road which was slow with heavy traffic and only got a glimpse of the turbine before Mirabelle saw a signpost saying, "Public Toilet".

'There – toilets!' she shrieked. 'That's the priority. The turbine will have to wait.'

'Okay and we can plan our arrival to the minute from here,' Apricot agreed as she parked the car.

Women!

'I'm in your hands, ladies. I'll stay and guard the car while you go first, then it's my turn.'

Apricot's timing worked perfectly, and she got them to their destination on the dot of ten past two. She parked the car between two other vehicles on the roadside and offered to stay there, listening to the radio.

'Are you sure? We might be some time,' Frank said.

'I'll be fine. I might just walk round the block, see if I can find the sea. I'll have my phone on if you need me,' Apricot replied.

Frank helped Mirabelle out of the car. While she straightened her dress, carefully chosen for the occasion, Frank reached across for his folded jacket before looking around at his surroundings. He imagined he could smell the sea air but the ocean wasn't visible from the front of the old-fashioned, semi-detached chalet bungalow. The garden path was overgrown with weeds and the green paintwork on the front door was cracked and faded. Sea air's no good for paintwork, thought Frank, looking at the yellowed window frames which had probably once been white.

Wonder if she'll let you spruce the place up one day?

'Looks nice. Quaint, seaside shabby-chic,'

Mirabelle said. 'Are you ready?'

'As I'll ever be.'

'See you later, Apricot. Thanks again,' Mirabelle said and she took Frank's hand.

Gus opened the door and stiffly showed them into the sitting room, where various mismatched chairs had been arranged round an oblong coffee table. Frank's eyes went straight to an older woman in a maroon cardigan who sat in a carver chair next to Della. There she was - Maureen, his Mum.

Gus introduced Mr Thomas, the solicitor, who raised himself from an easy chair and held out a hand to Frank. He was surprisingly short and stocky when he stood.

Remind you of someone? I think I know who.

'Nice to meet you, Mr Roberts and who is this?' said the man, who looked like his post-rehab key worker, with his twitchy, bushy eyebrows.

'Pleased to meet you,' Frank said. He could feel Della and Maureen analysing him as he spoke. He pulled in his stomach muscles. 'And er... this is my good friend Mirabelle Jones.'

'Charmed,' said Mr Thomas.

Frank felt he was actually in an Agatha Christie a film. He and Mirabelle had watched "The Moving Finger" on TV recently and he was worried she might remember it too and giggle. Happily, she just smiled regally at the assembled company.

She's a trouper, this one.

'I think you've met my mother before,' Gus continued.

'Some time ago. Della, how are you?' Frank nodded.

'And this is my Aunt Maureen.'

Talk about dragging it out!

Maureen and Frank looked at each other for what felt to Frank like an eternity but was probably only seconds. Frank nodded and forced a smile. Neither said a word but nor did their gaze shift.

Eventually Gus indicated where Frank and Mirabelle should sit and suggested his mother made some tea.

'Can I help?' Mirabelle asked following Della to the little kitchen which she later told Frank was clean but old-fashioned.

After a bit of small talk about traffic and journeys and Lowestoft, over tea with homemade shortbread biscuits, Mr Thomas took to the floor. He stood up and delivered a long-winded presentation of what they all already knew about the DNA results as if he was lecturing students. Frank saw Maureen's feet twitch and Della frown. Gus fiddled with his watch.

Was that the watch Reg had left him?

Next to him, Frank could hear Mirabelle's calm, regular breathing and he decided to focus on that until the droning lecture on the significance of genetic testing came to a halt.

If only Frances Freeman was here as well!

Thankfully, Mr Thomas had another appointment and soon excused himself, saying they could call him at any time if there were any queries and he would be in touch with

Maureen soon. Even Maureen seemed to relax after he'd gone and they all shared some mutual amusement at the unusual little man. Mirabelle whispered to Frank that he seemed to belong to a different era.

'Might I have a few minutes on my own with Frank?' Maureen suddenly announced, looking steadily at her son.

Della had started to stack the tea things.

Gus checked with her. 'Mum?'

'Let's wash up and take a look at the back garden, Mirabelle. Gus, you can help too?' Della led the way out to the back of the house.

'I expect you have a lot of questions, Frank?' Maureen said.

'I have and to be honest, I don't know where to start... maybe at the beginning. What did you call me when I was born, because I don't imagine it was Frank?'

'I called you Christopher. For the first few weeks of your life, you were Christopher, my Christopher.'

'Christopher Hall, Chris,' Frank said. 'That sounds nice. What was my dad's name?'

'I'd rather not talk about him at the moment. Let's stick to you and me.'

'Why wouldn't you meet me before?'

'I'd let you go. I thought you'd been adopted and were having a good life. I didn't know how much you knew about me and I thought you'd hate me.'

'I was told nothing about you and I'm afraid my life's been complicated... anything but good,' Frank uttered. 'Not that I want to drag

173

you through all my stories at the moment. You're right. Let's focus on us in the here and now. If that goes well all the stories of the past will come tumbling out one day.'

'I like that idea.'

'It does mean we'll have to keep on meeting,' Frank said cautiously.

'I think we can manage that. Now tell me where exactly do you live and work and who is Mirabelle? Is that her car?'

'No, a friend drove us up. She's gone for a walk,' Frank answered. Gradually more questions followed from both sides. Frank answered as honestly and kindly as he could, exchanging facts rather than feelings, and he felt Maureen was doing the same. That pleased Frank, he wasn't ready for too much emotion from this old lady yet. Maureen kept her answers brief, casually changing the subject when it seemed she wanted to avoid an issue. She repeatedly expressed concern that the driving friend might need refreshment before they left.

When the others came back from the kitchen, Frank and Mirabelle reassured each other with familiar glances. All was well.

'I don't think we should stay much longer,' Frank said. 'Maureen must be tired but we can come back again soon.'

'That'd be lovely,' said Mirabelle. 'Shall I give Apricot a buzz and tell her we're ready to leave?'

'Yes, please do,' Maureen said. 'Ask her to come in and say hello. She might want a glass of water or to use the bathroom.'

'I wouldn't mind popping to the loo myself,' Frank said.

Frank heard Della grunt a little too loudly and saw her nudge Gus, as if to say, keep an eye on that one. Gus followed Frank into the hall and Frank managed to hold back from telling him he could manage his own flies, thank you very much. Gus was still lurking when Frank came out of the toilet.

'Think you've got it sorted, don't you?' Gus growled. 'I'm watching you. Mum and I don't want Maureen upset. Got it?'

'I've got it, Gus. Back off. I just want to get to know my mother. That can't be hard to believe. You and I are cousins now, whether you like it or not, how about meeting me in Ipswich before I go back to Felixstowe and we can talk?'

'Meet for a beer, you mean? Oh sorry, you don't drink do you?' Gus sniggered.

'I can handle a cola or a tonic, so you needn't worry about that.'

'How about tomorrow, 6 o'clock in The Salutation in Carr Street?'

The doorbell rang and Gus went to open the front door.

'You must be the driver,' Gus barked.

'Hello, yes, I'm Apricot. How do you do?' She smiled with a disarming confidence and stepped inside.

Frank realised he'd not seen her in full flow before as she moved towards the two older women in the front room.

'Now which one of you fine ladies is my fellow librarian? How kind of you to ask me in.'

'That would be me,' Maureen said from her chair. 'Can we offer you something? Tea or a cold drink?'

'A glass of water would be lovely, thank you. We mustn't stay long but I've been wondering if you and I might have met somewhere in the past, at a Library Association conference, perhaps?'

Frank stood back and watched Mirabelle smile. Della's eyes nearly popped out on stalks as Gus went to fetch a glass of water like an obedient servant.

'I used to be a member but I retired some years ago,' Maureen said. 'I can't think we've ever crossed paths. I stopped my membership when the association became the Chartered Institute – my successor at the library was very active in the Institute.'

The two ex-librarians bounced a few names back and forth and finally found a few names they both knew. They then chatted on as if they'd known each other for years and Maureen invited Apricot to return with Frank on his next visit. Apricot sipped her water then asked to use the bathroom.

'She's a character, isn't she?' Frank said to Maureen. 'Shall we get our diaries out and try to fix a date for another visit? I have to fit it round my work schedule I'm afraid.'

'There's no rush,' Della said sharply.

'It's a good idea to make sure Apricot is free to drive them. Frank tells me he doesn't drive,'

Maureen said calmly. 'I hope you will come back too, Mirabelle.'

'I'd love to, thanks. We can bring you the details of the Felixstowe Book Festival that Apricot mentioned. Some speakers can be accessed online. I see you still love books,' Mirabelle said, looking at the pile next to Maureen's chair and the laptop on the side table.

When Apricot returned, she suggested they leave to avoid the tea-time traffic.

'It's been lovely to meet you, Maureen, hasn't it Frank?' Mirabelle took Frank's hand as if to confirm their relationship and eventually they made their escape.

Frank offered to sit in the back on the way home because he wanted some quiet time to think over all that had happened on this momentous day. He closed his eyes and quietly played it over in his mind. Gus was as he expected although he thought there was potential for a relationship of sorts, *but goodness, Della was prickly!* He thought things would be alright building a relationship with Maureen however and was looking forward to their next visit. Mirabelle said she'd bring a picnic lunch next time to save Maureen any trouble and they could have it in the garden if the weather was nice. Spring was well on its way but you never quite knew what to expect of the English weather.

'You alright Frank?' Mirabelle asked, as they reached the main road.

'Fine thanks,' he replied. 'Why on earth did

you mention the Book Festival? We won't be able to take her.'

'I know, I was just trying to make a connection, show her we were interesting people.'

'Fair enough,' Frank grunted before lightening his tone. 'I must say I was amazed at what Apricot did to Maureen, it was like flicking a switch to turn on a different woman.'

'She cast one of her spells,' Mirabelle chuckled and Apricot laughed so enthusiastically, Frank was worried she'd lose concentration and crash the car.

He closed his eyes again and wondered how drinks with Gus would turn out. Mirabelle was interesting and so was Apricot but he doubted he could say the same about himself or Gus for that matter.

In bed that night Frank lay still, pretending to sleep.

'Trouble sleeping, love?' Mirabelle asked after a while.

'Sorry, I didn't want to disturb you.'

'I'm wide awake, too. Not surprised after a day like that. Do you want to talk?'

'Apricot was good, wasn't she?' Frank said. 'Her driving got better too as the day progressed.'

Mirabelle laughed, 'yes, she was absolutely brilliant. Why then do I feel a but coming on?'

'Does she really cast spells?' Frank asked.

CHAPTER 23

Frank walked through town to The Salutation just after 6 o'clock, wondering how things would go with Gus. He passed someone smoking in a shop doorway and breathed in the second-hand smoke. In his nervous state, Frank felt as if he could snatch the fag from the man's hand. The severe yearning for tobacco had been much less intense of late but had never gone away completely and this evening it was gripping. He imagined Mirabelle telling him to walk on. He turned away from the smoke and tried to breathe in fresher air.

'Stay calm, be kind to yourself and to Gus,' he whispered to himself, as he opened the door to the bar.

Gus was perched on a bar stool with an almost empty pint glass in his hand.

'What'll it be?' he asked as Frank approached.

'Tonic with ice and lemon please,' Frank replied, ignoring the predictable smirk on Gus's face.

Gus placed the order, adding another pint for himself and the two men moved across to a side table.

'Not driving, then?' Frank said.

'Sandra's coming for me and we'll get a meal together on the way home.'

'Nice,' said Frank. 'How long have you two been together?'

'Together for years, married for four.'

'Nice,' was all Frank could think of to say

again.

'You been married?'

'No.'

'What about Mirabelle, then, where does she fit in?'

'We've been friends for some months but only got together properly after the funeral.'

'The funeral, eh, nothing like a funeral for a bit of romance? After your money, I expect?' Gus sniggered.

'Certainly not,' Frank said, then he sharply changed the subject. 'I thought yesterday went well. Maureen relaxed after a while. It's good we'll be able to meet again - the first time was always going to be the hardest.'

'She was pretty washed out after you'd gone, so we didn't stay long. Mum didn't find it easy, either.'

'I could tell.'

'She's still very disturbed about the will, as are we all,' Gus announced, a little less harshly.

'I can understand. I want to try to make things better once probate is sorted but I can't say too much until we know what sort of money we're talking about. Miss Freeman seems to think it's more than anyone realises.'

'That the royal *we*, was it?' Gus asked, once again curt, before taking a huge gulp of beer, nearly finishing off his second pint.

'No, it's the family *we*. Like it or not, you and I are family and I think for Maureen's sake, we should try to behave like civilised human beings. It's no longer just about you and Della.

Now, would you like another pint?'

Gus looked taken aback, as if he wasn't used to anyone else taking the lead.

'Better make it a half or Sandra will be on at me. She wants me to cut down a bit.'

'Any particular reason?' Frank asked.

'It's not that I'm an alkie, if that's what you're thinking.'

'Wouldn't have crossed my mind. Just under the thumb, then?'

'You know nothing,' Gus barked. 'If you must know, we're still trying for a baby. That's what Dad's effing money should be paying for, not your early retirement.'

'Leave it out! I'll get you a half and then we'll talk this over quietly. Miss Freeman has advised me not to make any rash decisions but we don't all have to be losers in this situation.'

'Ta,' Gus said, when presented with his half. 'Frances said much the same to me when I asked about contesting the will. Said it would be hard to prove Dad was mentally incapacitated when he drew up the new one. The Parkinson's wasn't diagnosed until some time later and the dementia wasn't immediate.'

'Do you think the changes in that final will might be to do with his relationship with Della?' Frank asked cautiously.

'You know about how they got started, don't you?'

Frank nodded. 'Yes, and I know about Arthur. It's amazing the marriage to Reg survived.'

'Mum and Dad were friends before they

married but to be honest it never was a great romance. They were financially dependent on Arthur Trelawney right up to the boss's death a few years ago.'

Calm and kind seemed to be working, thought Frank as he listened, *and maybe the beer's helping things along.*

'I think after Arthur died, things changed for Dad, he got braver, stood up for himself more. Then he got ill and I think Mum felt sorry for him. The see-saw of their relationship got more balanced, I'd say, but by then it would have been too late for the will to be altered again. It was all a bit sad.'

'None of this can have been easy for you or Oliver,' Frank commented.

'What do you mean?' Gus looked startled.

'I mean the involvement of Oliver's father with Della.

'You really do know it all then?' Gus replied.

'Not everything. Tell me about Oliver.'

'We're like brothers, grew up together as youngsters. My mum was more of a mother to him than Arthur's snooty wife was.' Gus shrugged his shoulders 'It was only awkward for a while when Oliver inherited the house and became my boss. He tried to run the estate differently and give it a modern touch, even the changed the name to Lawn House.'

'Yes, that seems confusing,' Frank commented.

'Things didn't really work out,' Gus said.

'Is that why Oliver sold it and moved to Drift House?' Frank was getting more and more

your social life. Oh, sorry, I didn't mean... I know that's a bit of a moot point for Sandra and Gus at the moment.'

'So, everyone knows they're having difficulties now, do they?' Della asked. 'Why was I the last to find out?'

'It's only recently gone public. I do feel for them. Max has offered to put them in touch with some adoption agencies he's worked with, just for advice at this stage and so they know their options.'

'It makes me so sad. Gus could be the last in the genetic line of the Halls if he doesn't produce.'

'Don't think like that, Della, they're still in with a good chance. At least Sandra's that bit younger than Gus.'

'I suppose you're right,' Della commented. 'Come on, the tea's getting cold and I need some help eating up this cake.'

'We can never resist your cakes. Can you spare a slice for me to take home for Max?'

'Take what's left. I'll only get indigestion if I eat too much.'

'Is that still troubling you?' Jenny asked. 'Have you seen the doctor?'

'I'm going to the GP tomorrow. Don't mention it to Gus. He'll only worry,' Della replied. 'Celine's taking me because my car's going in for a service and MOT.'

'You could have asked me,' Jenny said. 'I've got the week off to be with the children.'

'No, you have some fun. I need to catch up with Celine anyway.'

'Actually, we were thinking of going to the library tomorrow in Ipswich. They've got another activity morning for the children and I thought it might be good for Jacob to have a more successful outing there. He goes to the library in Stowmarket but we've not been to the big one in Ipswich since the episode in January.'

'He's okay, isn't he?'

'He's fine. I want to go for my benefit. I can't stop feeling guilty, worrying I don't give the kids enough quality time because of work. The practice has been so busy, everyone seems to need to see a physio at the moment and I've been taking on more than I should. The little park near us is all I have time for and it's really boring as our main choice of entertainment. On top of that, I do need to finally put the whole episode with Tricia to bed.'

'You silly thing. You do lovely things with the children, just because one outing went wrong doesn't mean you should feel guilty,' Della said. 'How were you to know that manipulative vixen was in town?'

'Trouble is, it's not a one off, is it? It makes me concerned about my own judgement. It took me ages to get over leaving him with anyone after he got ill as a baby. Tricia let us down with her unreliable behaviour and then and blow me if she doesn't do it again. That day at the library brought it all back.'

'Well, Tricia is far away now and Celine's going to check that she's still behaving. James apparently has it under control. You'll soon be able to let your feelings settle. If not, it'll be me taking you to the doctor, for counselling.'

Della gave Jenny a motherly hug before showing her out. The pain under her right rib cage had been nagging her all afternoon and she went to the kitchen and took a dose of antacid before washing up. She leaned over the sink and was struck by a wave of nausea making her rush to the bathroom.

CHAPTER 25

'I saw Dr Harvey, the new one,' Della told Celine when she arrived back at the car. 'He looked like a schoolboy but was very nice. Thorough, I'd say. He asked if I'd been under any stress lately.'

'I hope you told him,' Celine said.

'I didn't want to trouble him, I said I just wanted tablets for my indigestion.'

'And he gave you a prescription?'

'Yes. Can we pop to the chemist on the way home?'

'Course, but what else did he say?'

'He asked me how much alcohol I drank. What a cheek! Anyway, he found a tender spot in my tummy and now he wants me to have blood tests and a scan.'

'That's good. Thorough, as you said.' Celine smiled. 'What's he looking for?'

'He's wondering about gallstones but other things needed to be excluded.'

'What, like an ulcer?' Celine started to look concerned.

'Yes, that sort of thing. Of course, it might just be stress after everything that's happened. Don't say anything to Gus.'

'Okay, but make sure you tell him when you're ready. I'll have to drop you off smartish once we've got your medication. I'm afraid Alfie needs to be let out before I pick up the girls from school. Lynn's working away this week so I'm doing everything.'

Della got her prescription and never got

round to asking Celine how Tricia was doing.

Her own car was soon back on the road with a good-to-go MOT certificate tucked into its documents file. Two days later Della drove herself to the local outreach clinic for the blood tests and was surprised when she returned home to find a letter already on the doormat. She was booked in for an abdominal ultrasound scan the following week.

That was quick, she thought, *they must have had a cancellation.* She wouldn't tell Gus or anyone else for now. Gus had enough on his plate, Celine was busy and Jenny would be back at work after her break with the children. She could take herself.

She decided to open her medication, having put it off for the last few days. She took the first tablet without even reading the instructions; if they worked quickly, she might even be able to cancel the scan.

No such luck, after a week of disturbed nights Della drove herself to the Ipswich Hospital for the scan. She went early to ensure a car parking space and made herself comfortable in the out-patient waiting area. She took a paperback book from her bag to help pass the time but couldn't concentrate. She dug out her appointment letter and double-checked the details and the time. She'd had an early, light breakfast as instructed and now longed for a cup of tea but knew she shouldn't have anything else until after the scan.

She watched people come and go; all shapes and sizes, all colours and creeds, and she wondered what they all were there for. Some looked fit and well and some looked so poorly she felt like a fraud when all she had was a bit of tummy ache. A woman walked down the corridor pushing a trolley with squeaky wheels which stopped when she paused to talk to first one and then another waiting victim. Not wanting to enter into conversation with anyone, Della kept her head down. The squeaks came nearer and she took a quick a peep at the offending trolley. Laden with newspapers and refreshments, it looked heavy to push and she read a sign stuck on the side saying Ipswich Hospital Volunteers.

Della looked up at the woman pushing it. She was tall and slim in neatly tailored beige trousers, and wore a dark blue tabard over a fitted, pale blue jumper. She must have been in her late fifties, maybe sixty, with hair very obviously dyed in a most unnatural colour. It wasn't exactly golden, but more apricot in colour. The woman was smiling at the people she drifted past and every now and then she repeated rehearsed lines, 'Soft drinks and snacks, magazines or papers. Tea and coffee are available at the kiosk by the door.'

Della's breath caught and she started to cough. The woman turned to her and held out a bottle of water.

'Are you alright? Would this help?' she asked then gave out a funny squeal. 'Oh, my goodness, it's Della, isn't it? Remember me?

Apricot.'

'Apricot, yes of course, Mirabelle and Frank's friend. Fancy seeing you here,' Della said, keeping her voice down, conscious of almost everyone in the waiting area looking her way.

'I volunteer here once a week. I like to do my bit,' Apricot replied. 'I know it's not my business but you look flushed. Are you quite alright? Are you here alone?'

'I'm fine, just here for a routine check up.'

'Would you like me to sit with you while you wait?' Apricot said and without waiting for an answer, she sat down next to Della.

'I'm due in soon, please don't worry,' Della said.

'They always run late and my feet could do with a rest, to be honest. Who are you seeing?'

'I'm just having a routine scan.'

'That's good, nothing serious then. How's your lovely sister-in-law? I did enjoy meeting her. I'm so looking forward to having a longer chat next time and I must say Lowestoft was more interesting than I expected.'

'I'm not sure I'd agree but yes, Maureen's doing quite well, considering all the upset.'

'Yes, of course. I'm so sorry, I didn't say my condolences about your loss.'

'Why should you? You didn't know Reg and you don't know us,' Della replied starkly.

'It was a strange day for everyone, meeting like that. I'm sure it'll get easier.' Apricot said. 'I know Frank and Mirabelle are keen to get to know you all.'

Della was wondering how to reply when her

name was called out. 'Mrs Hall, Della Hall, this way please. We're in Room 2.'

'Goodbye, Apricot,' Della said firmly and followed the radiology nurse to the scanning room.

When she emerged almost an hour later, Della scanned the corridors carefully, checking to see whether Apricot was lurking. She thought she heard her voice bossing people about behind the kiosk so took a long way round to the main exit, just in case. She went to the pay machine and stuffed her money in with just minutes to spare before the fee went up. At least she'd remembered to take pound coins and this machine gave change. She held her tummy, it was sore after all the prodding and poking and she thought how awful it was to have to pay for pain. In the car, she sucked on a peppermint flavoured antacid tablet and paused to get her breath.

Well, that's me sorted for the next few weeks, she thought, as she read an instruction leaflet she'd been handed. Low fat diet, no pastry or cakes, no wine, and lose a bit of weight before potential surgery. *At least they're not keeping me waiting to sort this out and Dr Harvey will have the full result by the end of the week. The NHS is a marvel.*

Della drove home, got out of the car and vomited on her front step. She managed to throw a bucket of water over the mess before going to lie down, relieved she'd not had much to eat that morning.

She woke from a doze to hear Gus letting himself in the front door.

'Mum, you okay. What's that mess on the path, it stinks?'

'Just coming.' Della struggled to her feet and met him in the hallway. 'I think I've eaten something that'd gone off.'

'You do look a bit ropey, come and sit down. Where've you been, I've been calling you?'

'Just out,' she said.

'What are you up to? I've come to tell you we've got the grant of probate so we can get on now with sorting things out. Mum, are you sure you're alright?'

'Not really, I've had a bit of a morning actually.'

'I think you'd better tell me about it. I'm listening.'

'I've been getting indigestion for a while and I've just got back from a scan appointment at the hospital.'

'Why on earth didn't you tell me? What is it? Oh, Mum it's not... you know what? Tell me it's not cancer!'

'No, love, they're pretty sure it's not. But I have multiple gallstones and one is very near the pancreas, causing inflammation, so they don't want to leave it. They showed me a picture, very interesting. Anyway, they've given me a preliminary date for an operation.'

'Hope it's not when we're hoping to go to see Maureen again. You said you wanted us all to keep in touch,' Gus said.

'You'll have to go on your own or take

195

Sandra.'

'What... and leave you alone in hospital? No, we'll rearrange. Perhaps we should go earlier, before your op. Oh, Mum, are you okay about this? You hate hospitals.'

'I know, but I don't think I've got much choice. I have to see Dr Harvey at the end of the week and he'll go through the blood results and talk me through what's going to be done.'

'Will you let me come with you?' Gus asked.

Della surprised herself by agreeing.

'I'll clean the step before I go back to work. Do you need me to get you anything? Shall I call Celine to come and sit with you?'

'She's busy and I'll be fine. I just need this prescription. It'll be a painkiller and some antibiotics for the inflammation. I have to take them until the op.'

'Why didn't you collect them from the hospital pharmacy?'

'I wanted to get out of there quickly. I didn't want to bump into that Apricot woman who was working in the volunteer shop.'

'You mean Apricot with the stirring voice and the hair?'

'The very same! I could have done without her seeing me, I can tell you,' Della said. 'I'll just have some water to drink and maybe a piece of toast later but Gus, I don't think I'll feel up to coming to Lowestoft with you before the op. You go and take Sandra like I said.'

'We could just talk to Maureen on the phone. Mind you, I bet Frank goes up again soon and gets his feet nicely under her table.'

Della groaned.

'It's not that much of a problem, Mum.'

'The pain's coming back,' she gasped.

'I'll go and get your medication and come straight back. If you're no better soon, I'll call that GP.'

The next day Dr Harvey admitted Della to hospital. When Gus and Sandra visited, she was on a drip and seemed to make no sense, under the influence of strong painkillers. She rambled on about stamps and strange visits from Chinese men. She thought Gus was Oliver, and Sandra was Oliver's first wife, Alexis.

'How are the twins?' she asked in a slurred voice. 'They must be nearly six months now? Where's my Reg? Thought he and Gus would be here by now.'

'Mum, it's me, I'm here, with Sandra, not Alexis. Alexis isn't with us anymore and nor is Dad, remember?'

Della tried to sit up but fell back with a groan.

'Did you bring the stamps, Alexis?' she asked Sandra.

'I don't have them but they're safe, don't worry,' Sandra replied kindly. 'Shall I call the nurse?'

Gus nodded and held his mother's hand while Sandra scurried off.

'Reg has hidden the stamps,' Della said.

'No, Mum, Dad's not here anymore. The stamps are yours now and they're safe. They're away being valued remember?'

'You must stop them. The man's going to steal them and take them back to China in a boat. Has Reg gone to China too?'

'No one's going to China.'

'Not even Alexis?'

'No, Mum.'

Della closed her eyes.

'Nurse is coming soon,' Sandra whispered as she resumed her place next to Gus. 'She says just humour her for now, it's the drugs talking.'

'Let's hope so. Even with dementia, Dad made more sense than this,' Gus commented.

'To be fair, Reg didn't say much at all did he?' Sandra smiled at the memory.

'Are you laughing at me?' Della shouted, even though her eyes were shut.

The nurse arrived at that moment. She spoke to Della in a beautifully calm voice and then explained to Gus that they'd change her painkillers and once she was rehydrated, the confusion would settle. Then they were very keen to get her into surgery to remove the offending gallstones and clear the blocked tubes.'

'Is it my imagination but does she look a bit yellow?' Sandra asked.

'Yes, the flow of bile is being obstructed by the stones and that's why she needs surgery. They'll remove the gall bladder and check the bile ducts for residual stones.'

'And that'll settle the pain and the inflammation?' asked Gus.

'That's the idea, but we'll have to keep a

decision with Mirabelle before contacting Gus. When going to pick up the phone, he dithered and decided to wait until he saw her face-to-face but then he couldn't sit still. He fidgeted, paced the floor, looked in the mirror, then re-read Frances Freeman's letter before getting his holdall out to start packing for the next day. He hid the envelope in the base of his bag beneath a covering of clothes then zipped it up. He put on his jacket and set off for a walk to the supermarket next and on the way, passed a corner shop. Once again, he had that yearning for a cigarette.

No, Frank, you made a promise to Mirabelle. Keep walking.

At the supermarket, he bought three Easter eggs, a fancy, decorated one for Mirabelle and two plainer ones for Maureen and Apricot. They were all off to see Maureen that weekend. Frank drifted past the wine department thinking most people would celebrate with champagne. He looked at an alcohol-free, sparkling wine and sighed, it would be asking for trouble to even get a hint of the taste. He bought himself a bottle of cola, a nice rib eye steak, a jar of Dijon mustard and some posh, pre-prepared potatoes as a treat for his tea. For dessert, he chose a cream cake from the patisserie next door.

A rich man's feast!

The voice seemed to have a new cynical edge to it as he unpacked the shopping in the kitchen.

'Shut up, clever Dick,' he said out loud. After

all, he was allowed to have some treats. Now he just hoped he was alone in the house and had the oven to himself so he could eat early before choir practice at seven thirty. Perhaps he'd leave the cream cake until after choir - the cream might clog his vocal cords and he wanted to impress the choirmaster. Surely Carlos wouldn't touch it if he left it in the pack and labelled it.

That night, Frank couldn't sleep. He wondered if the strident singing had wound him up too much, or was it the cream cake lying heavy in his stomach? More likely it was the contents of the letter from the solicitor and the anticipation of telling Mirabelle about it. Talking about the money to her would make it real and not just the dream he'd been toying with for weeks. He was relieved when his alarm finally went off and he could face the day. He could always close his eyes and snooze on the bus or maybe suggest an afternoon nap with Mirabelle.

When she opened the door to him, Frank dropped his holdall and the bulging shopping bag on the doorstep and hugged Mirabelle in the tightest bear hug he could get away with without suffocating her.

'Frank, what's got into you?' she gasped. 'I can hardly breathe.'

'Sorry, love, just so pleased to see you,' he said letting go and following her inside. 'These are for the weekend.'

'All for me? You must be kidding. I'll be fat

said.

'I suppose there's no reason you should. She's had her gall bladder out and they found a pancreatic cyst. They drained it but now the pancreas is playing up again and she's gone back in.'

'Is it serious?'

'Could be, especially if she gets full-blown pancreatitis. Poor Gus is very worried.'

'I'll call him when I get back. I do try to make an effort with him, you know.'

'It would make me happy if you two were to get along.'

'I need to talk about the money. Can I run a few thoughts by you?' Frank asked.

'Okay, what is it? You know I'm going to be just fine with my £10,000.'

'Are you sure?' Frank queried.

'Yes, I'm not buying a car as someone suggested, this other hip is getting worse and then there's my knee that needs doing so I've decided a mobility scooter would suit me better. That'll get me to the library and the shops and if I need to go any further, I'll order a taxi.'

'But you will let me know if you need anything won't you? I was wondering if I could help you spruce up the house and garden. Mirabelle could help too, if you want. She's very artistic, you know.'

'She's certainly colourful, I'll give you that. Her style might not be mine though, Maureen chuckled. 'We'll see.'

'Fair enough. You think about it. I'd really

like to offer Gus and Sandra some money for their hospital bills. Has Della told you their situation?'

'Yes, such a shame. Gus is a proud man though.'

'I know, that's the problem, how do I offer to help without putting his back up? I'm not even sure how much these things cost but I know it's a lot. Could you do some digging for me? Maybe talk to Gus and Della when she's well enough, you know, sound them out. The first move might come better from you.'

'I'm sure Reg would have done things differently if he'd known they were trying for a baby. I still can't imagine what came over the man.'

'That's what I said to Mirabelle,' Frank said. 'That's why I want to make the offer. If things work out well, we could be talking about Reg's grandchild.'

'And Della's,' Maureen added.

'Yes, and I'll try to make things right with her too.'

'And you are sticking to your side of the bargain, aren't you, you are still sober?' Maureen asked.

'Yes, Mother, I am,' Frank grinned.

Maureen gave an embarrassed little laugh. 'That's the first time you've called me Mother.'

'Do you mind?' he asked.

'It sounded quite good. I don't mind Mum though. Next time you come, bring your gardening clothes, I think I'd like my son to spruce up the front garden for me.'

to rely on Apricot for lifts though and he would be happy to be designated driver when they went out together as a threesome. When he got back to the table, he reported the menu looked pretty decent and suggested they brought Apricot here for a thank-you meal sometime.

'If things go well, we could stay for food this evening, maybe see if Sandra and Gus want to join us?' Mirabelle suggested.

Frank was still pondering this idea when they arrived.

'You realise I haven't actually met Sandra before,' Mirabelle hissed, as they approached the table. She stayed seated as Frank stood up to greet the couple, and for a brief second, Frank thought she might leap to her feet and say, 'Salutations!' in one of her comedic voices. Happily, the moment passed. Sandra was on tonic water too and Gus requested beer, so Frank did the honours and ordered while Sandra and Mirabelle exchanged small talk. Both were smiling when Frank returned but he noticed Gus was looking serious and quiet.

Sandra was already geared up to discuss money. Gus had obviously spoken to Frances Freeman and he and Sandra must have already mulled over the issues and suggestions, just as Mirabelle and Frank had. Eventually Sandra looked straight at Frank.

'I don't think we should skirt about this much longer. Surely there's no need to be coy about it, we all know why we're here. You have the money Frank, we could do with some help and I'm not too proud to admit it. And although it's hard to believe, looking at his face, nor is Gus,' Sandra gave Gus a nudge and he managed a discreet nod, then a smile.

'Right, so we're ready to get real?' Frank said and he squeezed Mirabelle's hand.

Sandra presented a plan. 'We think the way to do is to have all future private hospital invoices sent directly to the main account of Reg's estate, which is currently still held by the solicitors. They will pay the bills out of the money left in the estate after you Frank, have received an interim payment to keep you going. It means you'll only get the residual when the terms of our treatment are over, so there'll be a delay before you get final closure. The plus side is that you won't have to handle the financial transactions yourself. Does all that make sense?'

'It sounds just about what Miss Freeman said to me. I'm in no great rush for the cash,' Frank said. 'She suggested we'd put a cap on the amount the hospital could claim and also how long this arrangement could go on. We have agreed a suitable ceiling amount and we both think this arrangement should only last 12 months.'

'Or less if you give birth in the meantime,' Mirabelle added.

'That sounds fair enough,' Sandra said

'Does anyone know what the solicitor's fees will be to handle this?' Mirabelle asked.

'She's drawing up a contract with terms and conditions as soon as we give her the go ahead,' Frank said.

Thursday and we used to joke about the nursery rhyme, you know, Thursday's child has far to go. Andy was a real little smiler. We always called him Thursday's child.'

'I hope for your sake he's still a smiler now,' Frank said. 'It's a good job I'm carrying on at work for a while. I was thinking I might just stay on until I've got my finances better arranged, I don't want to be out of pocket before I get the main settlement.'

'Whatever suits you,' Mirabelle commented blandly.

'Funny isn't it that Andy's first weekend here might have been my last one at work? As it turns out, it's good I've dragged my heels. I suppose you can have time alone with Andy and I can get my driving test ticked off.'

'Don't sound so despondent, everything will work out. This is just a pause, perhaps we were rushing it a bit.'

'I know, but I was excited. What if he doesn't like me? I've heard boys can be very protective of their mums.'

'He hasn't shown much tendency for that in the last 10 years, so why start now? He's in his late thirties, hardly a boy. It'll be fine,' Mirabelle said.

'Let's hope so. I'll come down to meet your Andy as soon as he's settled in,' Frank said. 'Order that carpet cleaner for the morning, while I wash the paintbrushes.'

In the car the next day, Frank asked Apricot if she'd known Andy before he went abroad.

She pulled a face but didn't answer.

'I think Mirabelle's a bit nervous,' Frank added.

'Excited, I expect, wants it to go well,' Apricot said.

'I wonder if she's ashamed of me?' Frank asked solemnly.

'I'm sure she's not - she loves you. She'd do anything for you.'

'You really think she loves me?' Frank sounded startled.

'Of course she does, hasn't she told you?'

'Only in passing, but then I don't suppose I've told her either.' Frank paused. 'I don't find these things easy. I hope it's not too late.'

'Don't be so daft. Maybe you should make your position clearer. It's very easy, just three little words.'

'Yes, I can do that. Now tell me about Andy.'

'I remember him as a chubby fair-haired chap, sporty, big muscles even as a lad. He was smiling and carefree when he set off to conquer the world. He was only meant to be gone a few months but then I gather he fell for some Australian, got a work permit and never came home.'

'I see. Unexpected, then,' Franks commented.

'Sure was. Plum's heart was broken for a while and then the blessed cat died. Well, that was nearly the end! I thought she'd given up completely but then she threw herself into her art, and painting became her salvation.'

'She's never told me that. I suppose it's good

Andy'll be here for her exhibition. I was going to help her prepare and set up. All this decorating has put the planning back a bit.'

'You know her well enough to realise she'll have it covered.'

'She seems a different person these days.' Frank sighed. 'Can the arrival of one son do that?'

'Just think about it. Your appearance in Maureen's world has changed your mother, but only for the better. Let dear old Plum rebuild her relationship with Andy and all you have to do is stand by her in case he lets her down.'

'Do you think he might? Here I am worrying about myself and it's Mirabelle I should be thinking about. We were thinking of taking Andy out for dinner when I come back to Ipswich. Might go to The Salutation - would you like to join us? We want to thank you for all your help and the lifts.'

'There's really no need, but yes, that would be lovely. Come on let's get this carpet cleaner before you disappear.'

On the drive back from the store, Frank watched Apricot's driving technique and road awareness. She was still a bit heavy on the pedals but despite that, she did seem a safe driver and not such a bad old fruit after all.

'I'm doing my theory test shortly,' he announced, out of the blue.

'Good luck with that. Have you done all the prep?'

'I think so. Any last minute tips?'

'Do online practice tests, read the questions carefully and stay calm. I did my test as an older person, so never fear - if I can pass, I'm sure you can.'

'I was never very good at exams so it won't be easy and Mirabelle's just presuming I'll pass.'

'Nothing worthwhile is ever easy,' Apricot smiled.

'Where've you two been? You've been gone ages!' Mirabelle snapped when they got back.

Frank raised his eyebrows at Apricot.

'They had to teach us how to use it,' Apricot said, peering through the living room door. 'What have you been up to?'

'Sorting my pictures out and labelling them.'

'Told you she'd have it under control,' Apricot said.

'Come on, we'd better get on before Frank runs off again,' Mirabelle said curtly. 'He can't keep away from that solicitor woman.'

She marched up the stairs and Frank watched her curvaceous buttocks wobbling within the constraints of some new purple, paisley dungarees. He knew she was doing it on purpose to bait him. Apricot nimbly followed with her smooth, featureless rear end, encased in camel twill and hardly moving at all.

You just wouldn't dare go there, would you?

'Frank, where are you with the machine?' Mirabelle shouted.

'Right here, love. Right behind you.'

CHAPTER 29

'I've passed. Can you believe it? I passed my theory test,' Frank called down the phone.

'Well done. Of course, you had a good teacher,' Mirabelle chuckled. 'Congratulations. Does that mean we can finally choose a car?'

'Hold your horses. There's still a small question of the practical to get through. I've just confirmed the dates for my final lessons and I've got an early cancellation date for the actual test. Trouble is, it's right after your art exhibition. I've booked some days off.'

'Let me put that in my diary, hang on while I get a pen.' She rustled in the distance. 'Gosh, that is close to the art show, Frank. And you're taking the test there in Felixstowe, not Ipswich.'

'Yes, I told you, that's where I've done all the practising so it makes sense. I've decided if I pass first time, which I bloody well should, having spent one and a half thousand bloody quid on it, I'll get on and hand in my notice. If I fail, I might work a bit longer to help pay for more lessons.'

'No pressure then, but you've said you know how to drive?'

'Yes, but it was ages ago when I used to drive Reg's Land Rover on the private roads round the estate and the lessons I've been having have been really good.'

'Don't tell me any more Frank, it worries me.'

'What do you mean?'

'Doing illegal things, like driving in the past without a licence,' she said.

'I only ever drove on private land a few times and I had a provisional licence. Reg was always with me.'

'Okay! And what about machinery at work? You know I worry about you there too.'

'We don't need to drive, and everything is very safe.'

'Good, but even so, you'd better flipping well pass your test, Frank.'

'I know, I intend to. Now how are things, you seem to be worrying? Is the house ready for the royal visit?' Frank asked.

'I think so and I've printed out the picture names and prices for the exhibition in good time. I do hope you can still get to the preview evening. Why on earth does everything happen at once?'

'That's life, Mirabelle, my dear. You've got this covered. I am very proud of you,' Frank said.

'Ah, really?'

'Yes really. You know I love you, don't you? I haven't said it enough. Sorry we were all a bit edgy the day with the carpet cleaner and then I left abruptly. I'm making sure you know how much I value us as a couple.'

'Us, I like the sound of that. You'll have to pass a test more often if this is the effect it has on you.'

'Just wait until I pass my practical,' he laughed. 'I'll show you how to celebrate. I need to hang up soon, I have to phone Gus before choir practice this evening. I'll call again tomorrow.'

'Okay, have fun. Oh Frank, was that contract all right?'

'Who knows,' he said. 'Best wait and see.'

It was the very next day that Gus called Frank and they both agreed the contract was acceptable, especially as the next hospital bill was due in soon. Della had now been informed and although she still wasn't on top form, or maybe because she wasn't, she agreed, all too easily that it was a practical solution. Everything was turning out right for once in his life.

CHAPTER 30

Frank had booked a table for four people to have dinner and he arrived at Mirabelle's house a couple of hours early, wearing his best new shirt for the occasion. He'd had his hair trimmed at the barbers, determined to make a good impression on his first meeting with Andy. He decided not to use his key but knocked on the door and waited, presuming an excited Mirabelle would rush to open it.

After a longer wait than felt comfortable, the door swung open. A tall, well-built man with a glowing suntan stood behind it, dressed in tight black running shorts and a grey singlet.

'Andy?' Frank said, holding out his hand to be shaken. 'I'm Frank.'

The hand was ignored.

Frank could hardly look the younger man in the face. His eyes were drawn to the broad shoulders and biceps, both upper limbs and torso densely covered in elaborate tattoos.

'Hi, pleased to meet you I guess, come in,' Andy said with only the slightest hint of an Australian accent and not as harsh as Mirabelle had suggested when she'd reported Andy's arrival. She'd said she could hardly recognise his voice and seemed quite upset that he no longer looked or sounded like her little boy.

Frank followed him down the hall and spotted a crocodile tattooed on one shoulder and a reclining naked man on the other.

'Sorry about the sweaty gear, mate, just

been for a run,' Andy said. 'I'm going to take a shower. Mum's in the kitchen. Back soon, then we'll have a beer.'

Mirabelle was emptying the dishwasher.

'Hello, love, you've met him, then? What do you think?' she said clattering her way through the utensil drawer.

'We hardly met. Handsome lad though. Obviously works out. How are you finding it, having him home again?' Frank went to kiss her but she'd already turned away.

'He'll be down soon,' she said looking flustered. 'He'll be changing for dinner. He's grand, isn't he? I can't keep up with his food and beer intake, he wants loads of protein, all pulses, eggs and fish, no meat.'

'Not even paddle fish?' Frank said, in the vain hope a little teasing would brighten Mirabelle.

'Any fish, so long as it's fresh,' she replied. 'And he runs and does yoga every day, says it's good for his mental state. I can't keep up with the washing either.'

'He's only been here a few days, surely he's not worn you out already? Ask him to help.'

'I want to spoil him a bit. I have ten years to make up for,' Mirabelle said.

'Sit down and let me make you a cup of tea,' Frank offered. He heard heavy footsteps on the staircase; the lad was on his way down.

'Well, aren't you two cosy?' Andy jibed. 'Just having tea? I'll have a beer thanks Mum.'

Mirabelle jumped up from the kitchen table and got a beer from the fridge.

'Driving, are you, Frank?' Andy blurted as he pinged the ring of his can and beer dripped onto his denim shirt. 'Oh Mum, you've shaken this about too much.'

'Sorry, dear,' she said, and passed him a hanky to mop up.

'Actually, we're walking to the restaurant,' Frank said. 'Apricot will meet us there.'

'You didn't say the old dragon was coming. Why on earth is she invited?'

'She's been very kind to us, Andy. It's a long-standing arrangement,' Mirabelle told him.

'We wanted to thank her for helping us with transport and it'll be nice to give her an outing,' Frank said.

'She doesn't approve of me or my lifestyle - never did in the old days and certainly won't now. She can be worse than you Mum – talk about judgemental.'

'Don't say that, Andy dear, you must admit you were a bit wild before you left. I think Apricot was cross with you for abandoning me. I was too at first but now I understand a bit more. I'm getting used to things being different and I'm glad we've been able to talk face to face,' Mirabelle said.

Frank tried to read between the lines.

'How many times! I didn't abandon you, I just had to get out of this stifling place and start my real life,' Andy said raising his voice.

'I know, I know, calm down, but I was in a bad place after your dad left and you bringing random young ladies home every night wasn't helping.'

'Let's not go over that again, I told you I was over-compensating because I was miserable. I couldn't be myself here in Ipswich with all the boys from school and the lads from the football club watching my every move.'

The fridge door squeaked as Andy opened it again and helped himself to another can of beer.

'Let's go into the other room,' Mirabelle suggested.

'What's going on?' Frank whispered as she steered him out of the kitchen.

'I'll tell you later. I thought he was going to be all right about tonight but he's been exchanging emails with his boss in Australia and something's happened. I think he might have been sacked.'

'That's tough. No wonder he's like a balloon about to burst. Shall we cancel?' Frank suggested quietly.

'Going out might do him good. He's been very moody since he arrived,' she whispered back, 'I thought it was jet lag but now something else has tipped him over.'

'We'll ask him what he wants to do,' Frank said, just as Andy joined them, with a large packet of crisps in one hand and a beer in the other.

'Talking behind my back?' he snarled.

'Your mother was just saying you've not had a good day,' Frank replied. 'Shall we cancel tonight's table? We can always rearrange it.'

Andy chomped on his crisps, dropping crumbs and saying nothing.

'Or we can phone Apricot and ask her if she minds just us three going? That would be easier for you,' Mirabelle said.

'Tell you what, you two go out with Apricot and I'll stay here. I could do with some peace and time to think. I'll find something to watch on Netflix and get a takeaway. No point me spoiling everyone's evening.'

'I don't want to leave you if you're feeling down, Andy. Frank and I don't mind cancelling do we Frank?'

'Just go,' Andy snapped and left the room.

'Is he okay to leave?' Frank asked. 'Maybe we should try to get him to talk.'

'Perhaps in the morning. Let's just go out, we needn't be long and I could do with an outing. I want to be able to talk to you, Frank. There's lots to discuss.'

They found Andy sulking in the hallway, looking for a takeaway menu. He nudged the stacked boxes of pictures waiting to go to the exhibition.

'Careful,' Mirabelle said.

'I'm not hurting them; it was an accident. Stop nagging,' he barked, then changed his tone to ask if he could use her card to order the takeaway.

Mirabelle put on her coat and sighed. Frank shook his head.

'No need, here's a twenty pound note you can take,' Frank said.

He followed Andy back to the living room where in a voice too low for Mirabelle to hear, he said, 'We'll not be late. Do whatever thinking you have to do but try to be civil to your mother when we return. I'm looking forward to getting to know you properly, Andy. I want us to trust each other for Mirabelle's sake if nothing else.'

Returning to the hallway, Frank felt his heart thumping. He hoped he hadn't sounded too overbearing but this young man needed to pull his head in. He took Mirabelle by the hand and led her out of the front door into the cool evening air and took a deep breath.

'I hope he'll be alright,' she said.

'He'll be fine.'

'I am worried about him. He seems to have gone off the rails. The split from his partner has shaken him and he's made some bad mistakes at work. That's why he's been sacked.'

'Must have been pretty serious to get the sack,' Frank said.

'He forged his time sheets to get some extra money. Eric had thrown him out of the flat they shared and he needed a rental deposit for a new place.'

'Eric?' Frank queried with raised eyebrows.

'Yes, Eric,' Mirabelle replied.

'Did you know?'

'I'm sure he said his partner's name was Erica and they'd met at a yoga class. I must have heard what I wanted to hear. He was always one for the ladies before he left.'

'Classic cover up,' Frank commented. 'Or trying to convince himself.'

'A bit of both, by the sounds of it. He came

out in his second year in Australia but he's only just told me, his mother, this week.' Mirabelle choked back a sob.

'Don't cry, you'll smudge your make-up. It's not the end of the world. We can talk to him later or else in the morning and try to understand. We've both had hard times and hit the depths. If we can support him through this, he will survive.'

'You're a fine man, Frank Roberts,' she smiled. 'I'm not upset because he's gay, I'm upset because he's unhappy. Can we change the subject now? There's Apricot parking her car over there, please keep the conversation vague when it comes to Andy and concentrate on your news, you know, stuff about Gus and Maureen.'

'Oh yes, because that's so straightforward,' Frank laughed.

'Okay, we'll stick to small talk about the choir and your driving test.'

'Or your art show and future plans for Maureen's garden.'

'Deal.'

When they got home, there were four more empty cans of extra strong lager on the table and the debris of a half-eaten Chinese meal was spread around the front room. The lights were on but the house was quiet and there was no sign of Andy.

'He'll have gone to bed,' Frank said.

'It's only half past nine, how long does jet lag last?' Mirabelle retorted. 'Oh goodness, there's chow mein trodden into the carpet. Get a damp cloth, Frank, while I pop upstairs and check.'

Frank cleaned the mess then followed Mirabelle up the stairs. She'd stopped on the landing and was outside Andy's room, listening to the snores coming from within. She shrugged her shoulders at the picture of Ricky the cat. Mirabelle pushed the door open a crack and they both peeped in. The light shining from the landing was just enough to reveal Andy, fully clothed, sprawled on his front across his bed. His snoring turned to a purr and he sighed in his sleep.

'Leave him, he's breathing all right. Keep the door ajar then we can look in again later,' Frank whispered.

'What if he's sick and inhales vomit? This is worse than having a teenager in the house again,' Mirabelle said when they were back downstairs. 'A poor end to such a nice evening. Thanks for dinner, I think Apricot enjoyed it.'

'Yes, it was good, and on the whole, we managed to avoid discussing anything complicated. She seems very taken with Maureen, even though we tried not to talk too much about her,' Frank said. 'Are you putting the kettle on?'

'Can you do it, love? I'll have camomile tea please. There's some lemon and ginger there if you'd prefer.'

They sat on the settee, switched on the television and supped their tea while waiting for the ten o'clock news.

'You're quiet, Mirabelle,' Frank commented.

'Everything alright?'

'I'm completely whacked and worried sick, to be honest. I don't think Andy'll be going back to Australia now, what with no job and no Eric to return to. He really needs my help but it's not going to be easy.'

'Does he always drink like that?' Frank asked.

'He didn't used to but it's been every day since he got here,' Mirabelle said.

'Do you want me to speak to him? It's not fair on you, I can hear the way he talks to you when he's been drinking and I don't like it,' Frank said.

'Please don't say anything. I'll just keep an eye... perhaps he'll settle down.'

Andy didn't get up until midday. He came downstairs wearing his running gear, just as Frank was coming in through the back door.

'You're not going straight out, are you? Let me make you some brunch,' Mirabelle suggested.

'Coffee'll do. Where's your man been?' Andy said with a thick, hung-over voice and not even looking at Frank.

'Just putting the rubbish out. You left a bit of a mess last night, and my goodness, you stink of stale beer. Some eggs might do you good.'

'Coffee and a run will fix me. I just need to clear my head.'

'So that's how it works is it, we clear up your mess and you clear your head?' Frank said.

'It's fine, Frank, leave it. I'll talk to him later.'

'Eff off, you two,' Andy said, slamming the door.

Mirabelle shuddered, which said more than words. She put her hand up to stop Frank following him. Frank picked up the newspaper and went to sit on his own in the back yard. He looked at the bulbs coming through and listened to check Mirabelle was okay in the kitchen. After a while, she came to him in the garden.

'It's warmer than I thought out here,' she said, as if nothing had happened. 'I hope the weather stays nice for my exhibition - it might bring more people out.'

'Are you going to make him apologise for that?' Frank said, still looking at the paper.'

'When the time's right,' she replied.

'Oh, Mirabelle, this isn't good. At the very least, you must make the grumpy so-and-so help at your show to make some amends. I told you last night I have to go back to Felixstowe straight after setting up.'

'I really hoped you'd stay for the launch evening,' Mirabelle said sadly.

'Sorry, love, but I've got to squeeze in some more lessons. I've been so lucky getting a cancellation date for my test and if I don't take it, I might be waiting ages.'

'Okay. I can tell you're getting anxious but please don't call Andy grumpy, he's just troubled at the moment.'

'He reminds me of myself as a younger man and I don't like that memory. I've only been here 24 hours and he's stirring me up.'

'I'm sorry. I hadn't thought about how he must be affecting you. Is it a problem having so much alcohol in the house?' she asked.

'Maybe, but it's more about how he looks at me and how presumptuous and downright rude he is with you.'

'You mean you don't like him,' Mirabelle said even more sadly. 'I don't always like him but I do love him. He's my only son and I'd do anything for him to be happy, now I have him back.'

'Anything?' Frank raised his eyebrows.

'You know what I mean. Can we change the subject and enjoy our time together while he's out? Then I'll make a frittata for all of us to eat together.'

'So, when do we get access to hang the paintings? Is there anything else we need to do?'

'We can go in the day after tomorrow. The timing's tight for these temporary shows at the library but I think I'm okay with it. I've already sent out the formal invitations to the private viewing. The protocol at these events is to offer a glass of fizz to each guest but of course we can't charge for it.'

'Who's providing the wine?' Frank asked.

'Me. It's what you do on these occasions. Don't worry, I haven't invited too many.'

'You're the boss. Let's hope you sell enough paintings to cover costs.'

'It's alright, I have a rich boyfriend.' Mirabelle smiled.

'How are we hanging them? Will I need to take hammers and screwdrivers?' Frank responded flatly.

'That's very thoughtful but the library has fixed rails to hang them from and the brass hooks are provided. We might just need to adjust the cord lengths.'

'Somebody might nick them if they're just hung on hooks,' Frank said.

'I doubt it but there is a security person on site now.'

'One good result from Jacob's little scare, I suppose.'

'Yes and I'm happy with the hanging. We can stick the titles and price cards on the rail with some double-sided tape.'

'They have titles! I can see you have thought of everything,' Frank smiled and patted Mirabelle's knee.

'Nearly everything. Of course they have titles but I'm a bit worried about payments if I sell any.'

'You mean when?'

'I've got some red dots just in case but the library people say I have to deal with payments myself. I'm hoping people will write cheques or pay by cash.'

Andy had just arrived through the back gate and stood listening with a smirk on his face.

'No one writes cheques these days. You'll have to ask for online bank transfers,' he blurted.

Frank couldn't hold back. 'And hello to you too Andy. Do you have something to say to your mother?'

'I said I'd deal with it,' Mirabelle snapped and leaned away from Frank. 'We were talking about payments. Online transfers mean giving out my bank details.'

'That's what you have to do to make a sale, Mum. Suck it up,' Andy said.

'Okay, calm down, I can understand your concern, Mirabelle, but you'll only give your details to genuine buyers, it'll be fine,' Frank reassured.

'I'll be glad when this is all over. At least Apricot will be there to help once you've gone home, Frank,' Mirabelle said.

'Leaving the sinking ship, eh?' Andy laughed. 'I expect Mum'll ask me to help.'

'Feeling brighter, are we?' Frank chipped back. 'I blooming well hope you do help. Your mother's put a lot of effort into this show and you should be proud.'

'Stop it, you two. You're as bad as each other. Frank has a lot on in the next couple of weeks, Andy, as well as work and an important choir rehearsal,' Mirabelle replied.

'Choir, what are you, some sort of God squad choirboy? And you look old enough to be retired so what's with the work?' Andy sneered.

'I told you Frank works at the warehouses at the docks but he's going to stop soon, aren't you love?'

'We'll see. I'm delaying early retirement for now.' Frank emphasised the early.

'Really? But I thought it was all going

ahead.' Mirabelle was now puzzled.

'We'll talk later,' Frank said.

'Anyway, his choir is a very accomplished group of community singers. They're doing a concert tour in Suffolk and Norfolk soon and that's why he has to rehearse. Some people know how to use their time constructively,' Mirabelle commented.

'Meaning?' Andy said.

'Nothing,' Mirabelle replied. 'I'm sure when you go back to Australia you can set up your yoga classes again and that'll help you feel more at ease with yourself while you look for another job.' Mirabelle tried to look encouraging but Frank could see she was failing miserably.

'Are you bloody deaf? I've told you - I can't go back to Australia.' Andy thumped a clenched fist fiercely on the wall and didn't even flinch.

'Okay, that'll do.' Frank stood up ready to challenge Andy. 'Your mother's just trying to be positive. Don't swear at her.'

'Sod you! I'm going for a shower. What time's lunch?'

'One thirty,' Mirabelle said in a subdued voice as Andy slammed the door and stormed upstairs.

'Look, I'm really worried about leaving you here alone with him. I might have to phone the boss. Maybe I can afford to take some extra days off.'

'But what about your driving test and the choir?'

'I'll just pop back for the rehearsal nights and rearrange some dates.'

'No, leave it. He's easier when you're not here, to be honest.'

'But do you feel safe?'

'Yes, of course I do, he's not that bad. I'll go and get lunch sorted. I'll call you when it's ready.'

This isn't good, Frankie boy, but what can you do... stay and make things worse or stick to your plan? Maybe get out of here. Mothers and sons can be complicated, speaking of which, it's about time you visited Maureen again.

Frank put his hands over his ears but couldn't stop the voice.

CHAPTER 31

In Docklands Road, Frank had no big decisions to make or difficult conversations to get involved with. When he wasn't working, he enjoyed the quiet of his room, listening to the radio or reading the paper. At work he kept himself to himself if he wanted solitude or could go to the canteen if he needed a chat. Yes, before he met Mirabelle, he'd had some lonely times but he hadn't felt stressed when he only had himself to think about.

Things were certainly changing now that he had a driving test, a partner, his mother and others to worry about. In fact, he had a growing list of people to consider and having to juggle time was becoming a challenge. He hardly managed to read the paper, let alone tackle the books he'd borrowed from Mirabelle. Choir and driving lessons were filling more space in his life than he'd expected and he was beginning to feel guilty at not visiting Maureen more. Mind you, she seemed happy with phone calls and didn't expect too much. After his driving course was done and dusted, he decided he'd try to give her more attention but for now the phone would have to do.

When Frank next rang Maureen, she wanted to hear all about the preview evening of Mirabelle's art show. Frank reported how well it had gone and how delighted Mirabelle was to have sold three of her pictures. He let on how difficult Andy had been in the build-up, finding it helpful to have someone to offload onto.

Andy's main job that evening was to offer one glass of Prosecco to each guest on arrival but he drank so much of it himself that they ran out and the latecomers just got sparkling water.

Frank admitted he was almost relieved to go back to Felixstowe and get away from Andy and Maureen sounded genuinely concerned. Frank regretted burdening her with his worries but she soon moved on and asked Frank to choose a picture for her, that was if Mirabelle had some left to sell at the end of the exhibition.

'Send me a photo of it first though so I can see if I like it,' she suggested wisely.

'I'm not going back to Ipswich for a while. I've got my driving test and then there's the choir,' Frank said.

'You sound as if you're avoiding seeing Mirabelle? Is it the son that's putting you off?' Maureen asked.

'I don't know... she's different when he's there. He and I seem to rub each other up the wrong way.'

'So it's him you're avoiding, while poor Mirabelle has to suffer him alone? If you and she are to have a future you need to sort that out, Frank. I thought you were about to move in?'

'I've got a lot on at the moment.'

'Sounds like an excuse,' Maureen said. 'Pass that driving test next week then get your backside to Ipswich and choose me a picture.'

'Yes, Mum,' Frank chuckled. 'Better go now.

I'll phone again soon.'

'Take care and good luck, son.'

Frank ended the call with a smile which faded away all too quickly.

It's good having a mother, isn't it? Have you forgotten all those years without her?

Next day, a letter arrived from Miss Freeman. The County Council and Social Services had confirmed receipt of the reclaimed money contributing to Reg's care fees and as it had been paid before a certain date, it meant there would be no additional penalties. Frank was a relieved that it was resolved but he also knew Oliver had contributed alongside Social Services and wondered if he needed to include Oliver in this financial maze. *Back to you, Miss Freeman*, he thought.

He checked his bank statement on the phone app, as he had done repeatedly that week, and gazed in on-going astonishment at the sum of money still sitting comfortably in his current account, even though at this rate, it might whittle down more quickly than he'd anticipated. He felt bad he'd not paid for the art show Prosecco but was also glad he hadn't, just for that lout, Andy to neck it all. Frank had already been informed by Miss Freeman that another bill of £600 for ultrasound scans had recently been paid to Sandra and Gus's private hospital, and another much larger payment was pending, for a procedure he didn't understand. Having more money wasn't as easy as it seemed.

He decided to phone Gus to check the hospital billing was correct. Of course it was but Frank still didn't fully understand what the procedures involved.

'And how is Sandra?' he asked, hoping for some simple answers, whereupon Gus went into a long and off-putting gynaecological description of what the poor woman was going through.

'Send her my best wishes. I'll keep track of the bills,' Frank replied. 'And Della?'

'Not great. She's still off her food and just can't get her energy back, it's quite a worry.'

'Maureen didn't say much that when I phoned her earlier,' Frank said.

'Mum won't have told her because she's pretending to be alright but I know she's not. She's a bit perkier now she's sold the stamps - at least she can afford some home help.'

'Will she accept help though? I thought independent was her middle name,' Frank said.

'She wouldn't have a stranger but Sandra thought about asking Celine, you know, Tricia's sister. She could go in a couple of times a week, more as a companion than a carer.'

'You're sure Celine's steadier than the sister?'

'No comparison,' Gus laughed. 'Celine is as reliable as they come.'

'You said you'd fill me in on Tricia one day.'

'How long have you got?' Gus sniggered. 'Actually, it's a story better told face-to-face, so

'Purple,' she admitted with a grin.

'It's great here. Why haven't we been before?' Frank asked, taking her hand.

'Too far to walk from my place and do you know what, we didn't have a car! Come on, coffee first before we visit the gardens. I think there's an arboretum too.'

'Okay, but what's that? The Reg Driver Centre? Funny name for a visitor centre and quite a coincidence, someone called Reg, me driving and now an arboretum to visit?'

'Serendipity. The stars have aligned to bring us here. Today will be a perfect day,' Mirabelle said.

'Oh look, the sign says it's an Education Centre and named after Reg Driver, a stalwart of the Ipswich British Legion. Obviously a local dignitary,' Frank said.

'I think my next cat will be called Reg, 'Mirabelle announced. 'The name seems to bring us good things.'

'Tell me you're not getting a cat!' Frank was horrified.

'Got you,' she laughed. 'Just kidding. I know you're not fond. There's the refreshment kiosk, I'll have a cappuccino please.'

'Sugar?' Frank asked.

'No, I've stopped. Andy says I need to lose weight.'

'You're fine as you are,' Frank said. 'You don't have to do everything Andy says.'

Mirabelle's face fell flat. 'Sometimes it's just easier to agree.'

'Let's go and sit on that bench,' Frank said,

carrying the coffees.' Are you warm enough? Now fill me in on what's been happening with Andy.'

'It's been okay really. He helped bank the money and clear up after the art show. In the end, after you'd gone, I sold five pictures as well as some cards.'

'That's brilliant, really good. And you made Andy proud?'

'He didn't say but I'm sure he was. One buyer paid in cash so I gave him a few notes to thank him for helping.'

'You are soft. He should have paid you after all the grief he's given you, let alone the fizz you said he drank that night.'

'Don't be mean, Frank, he's my boy and he's without an income at the moment. He's been in a poor way and I want to be able to help him,' Mirabelle replied.

'I just hope he appreciates it,' Frank said. 'He seemed to have enough money for his fancy lager when I was there. Is he still drinking heavily and every day?'

'Well, yes, but he says he runs it off. He doesn't like me to comment.'

'I don't think it works like that Mirabelle, you can't run alcohol off. I think I should speak to him about it. Does he know about my experience with such things? I might be able to prevent him getting dragged down like I was.'

'That's kind of you but I don't think he'd take advice from you.'

'Why? Because he doesn't like me, doesn't respect me?' Frank said.

'Not exactly... I think he's jealous. I don't think he wants to share me.'

'Oh, Mirabelle, that's not right. He's a grown man who's ignored you for years, he can't make up new rules now. I'll go gently but I'll have a word when the time feels right.'

'Don't, Frank. I said no, so stop. Fair enough, he drinks too much but at least he doesn't take drugs,' Mirabelle said, so sharply Frank almost spilled his coffee. He'd never heard that tone from her before and he didn't like it.

'If that's a dig at me, it's uncalled for. You know damn well alcohol alone can be a problem.' Frank managed to reply, struggling though he was to stay calm.

'I know my own son better than you do, so leave it Frank, I mean it.'

They finished their coffee in silence then set off to walk awkwardly towards the arboretum. For a moment earlier in the day, Frank had thought that this lovely park might be somewhere he'd like to spend more time. He could perhaps work there, as a volunteer or even get a paid job. The brief dream gradually faded away as they stared at the trees. Before long they turned for home.

Mirabelle set the kitchen table for three and put together a robust salad lunch. There was no sign of Andy.

'Are you sure he's not still in bed? Frank asked.

'I really don't know, Frank, I'm not his

keeper,' Mirabelle snapped. 'Water or tea?'

'Water's fine,' Frank said. 'I'm thinking of driving up to Lowestoft for the day tomorrow. Do you want to join me?'

'I have a few things I want to do here. I thought you might help me take some stuff to the tip tomorrow,' she said.

'I'd rather get off early to see my mother,' Frank replied.

'Go on your own then, if you're happy to drive that far as a new driver?'

'I'm sure I'll manage, thank you for caring. It's a straightforward route up the A12. I won't stay long.'

'Will you come back here after?'

'I might, if you'll have me?'

'Course I'll have you. Oh, Frank, no need to be like that.'

'Like what?'

'You know what. This is hard for me too you know.'

'You're being too soft on him. I've seen all those empty cans in the bin and heard how he talks to you. I'm worried.'

'About him or me?' she asked.

'You mainly but it's because of him. I really don't think I can move in with you if he's still here. There, I've said it.'

'I've been waiting for that. I'll not throw my own son out,' Mirabelle shouted.

'I wouldn't expect you to but surely you could set some house rules?' Frank replied. 'I seem to remember you had house rules when you ran this house as a B and B.'

'He is my son,' Mirabelle growled. Frank heard a helplessness in her voice.

'He's taking advantage. It's time to talk to him about his future plans. If anyone can help get him back on track, it's you Mirabelle. Look what you've done for me,' Frank said.

'This feels different,' she held her napkin to her mouth and Frank thought she might cry but she simply closed her eyes, breathed out quietly and then announced, 'We'll have a takeaway tonight. I don't feel like cooking.'

They picked at their lunch in silence. After washing up the two used salad plates, Frank asked if he could go on Mirabelle's computer in the front room to do some looking up. He went on AA route finder site and printed off the map to Maureen's place, then had a look at the Job Centre website, not for himself this time but for Andy. Shortly after, Mirabelle came into the room, quietly put on a paint splattered apron and went to her easel.

CHAPTER 33

Frank enjoyed the journeys he made over the following weeks to see Maureen. He grew in confidence as a driver and also in the conversations he had with his mum. They gradually heard each other's life stories and got to know how they each had turned out the way they were. Both had been denied an easy transition into adulthood and both could be equally guarded and cautious, after years of hidden hurt and secrets. As the barriers came down, they found they shared simple pleasures. They both liked cake, loved nature, gardens and music. Frank admitted that he preferred Maureen's gentle, still life watercolours to Mirabelle's bold mountains. Maureen was delighted Frank was reading more and soon took over from Mirabelle as his main book lender.

'You could just join a library, maybe the one where Apricot helps out?' Maureen suggested.

'I like borrowing your books.' Frank smiled and picked up a well-thumbed copy of Orwell's "1984" to take home.

Maureen nodded with an approving smile. 'Apricot phones me most weeks and sometimes she writes to me. She sends cuttings from the paper, she's awfully kind.'

'That's nice. Mirabelle thinks she's lonely.'

'Aloof people who exude confidence are often hiding something. She and Mirabelle are obviously good friends, Apricot often mentions her in her little notes. She says you've not been around as much lately?' Maureen said gently.

'I often pop over now I have the car but don't often stay. It's still not easy with Andy around. Let's just say he and I lock horns.'

'Ah, testosterone!' Maureen said.

'I suppose you're right. Having never had a child of my own I can't understand why she indulges him and lets him manipulate her so much. It's not like her.'

'Do you think he's really a bad egg or just a bit misguided?'

'He's nearly forty, so hardly a boy, but he behaves like a spoilt child.'

'Perhaps he missed having a father figure at a crucial time. You said he was a teenager when his father left.' Maureen commented. 'And has he found a job yet?'

'No, he's living off Mirabelle and drinking her money away,' Frank said.

'That's bound to worry you. Does it make you feel at risk? You know... of starting to drink again, because if it does, you need to deal with it. You could always go back to a support group if that's your concern.'

'No, I promise it's not that but I can just see him at the top of a slippery slope and having been there, I'd like to catch him before he falls,' Frank said.

'To help him or protect his mother? Or is it just to make you feel better?'

'Mirabelle asked me that too and I guess it's all three really. It makes me think about what Reg did for me when I was about Andy's age. Look at the difference having a supporter and mentor made to me. I feel inadequate that I can't do the same for him.'

'The circumstances are very different and maybe you're not the one to save him. Andy has to want to accept help, like you must have wanted to when Reg offered. Andy probably needs someone different to get through to him.'

'But who? Meanwhile, it's affecting my relationship with Mirabelle and I really can't move in if he's there.'

'Which just confirms you're not the one to be his saviour. You have to look after yourself first, Frank.'

'You can talk. How are things with the new carer?' Frank asked.

'She likes to be called a home companion. Cathy's her name. She's no spring chicken herself but she's very good. Prompt and not too chatty which suits me fine,' Maureen smirked. 'Three sessions a week works well for us both and I feel better now I have this helpline buzzer too.'

Maureen showed Frank her wristband with a red button on it.

'It's meant to be on your wrist not on the table,' Frank laughed and put it on for her.

'I'm still getting used to it. Enough of me, tell me about this choir of yours.'

'I feel a bit self-indulgent, gallivanting around the countryside on our summer tour next week. It means I'll not see Mirabelle for a while.'

'The break might do you good and give you both time to reflect. Tell me the itinerary then I can imagine what you're up to,' Maureen asked.

'There'll be four or five performances of World Music, spread over the fortnight, starting in Woodbridge and ending in Norwich.' Frank dug a leaflet out of his pocket and passed it to her. 'It means we'll get back to our own beds in Felixstowe each night, until after the last performance in Norwich and then we're all booked into a Premier Inn in the City. We're having a celebration dinner together in a nearby restaurant to mark the end of the season.'

'That sounds lovely. What on earth is World Music?'

'It just means songs from different countries to give a bit of variety. There'll be folk, blues, some classical and a bit of musical theatre thrown in.'

'I'd love to hear you. It says here you're going to Bungay a week on Wednesday, that's not far from here. They're bound to have wheelchair access in the Fisher Theatre. Can you find out and book a couple of tickets? I'll see if Cathy can take me.'

'Oh, it might be too much for you, don't worry. I don't think it's in the theatre, it's in a community hall,' Frank said.

'Oh really?' Maureen's cheeks flushed.

'What is it? Are you okay?' Frank asked.

'Nothing, no nothing at all, I just thought... oh never mind.'

'You really don't need to come. It won't be a smart place.'

'Stop being so bashful - a village hall's no problem. I'm coming and that's that. I might not have many opportunities to hear you perform again. Pass me the phone and I'll call Cathy. Look, there's a number here to book tickets in advance.'

'Oh God,' Frank said.

Oh God!

'Now who sounds like a spoilt child?' she said, as she dialled.

Frank prepared to return home soon after hearing, with considerable relief, that Cathy was otherwise engaged.

'Never mind, they'll be recording the Norwich concert so I'll get you a CD. I'll be getting one for Mirabelle too because she won't make it to any of the venues either.'

'That's a shame, never mind, I wish you luck and take care in that car,' Maureen said.

Bungay was second to last on the tour and the team were confident of a polished performance. Frank offered lifts to Olga and Sharon who eagerly took up the opportunity. The three of them arrived at the hall in good time. Frank spotted a tea-room across the way and asked his passengers to join him for some light refreshment before the concert. Olga and Sharon left the café before he did, to go and change for the performance. Frank meandered slowly after them, smiling at how women always made a bigger deal of getting dressed than men. Down the street, he spotted an orange car trying to reverse into a space marked disabled. The driver was making a meal of it and Frank wondered if he should offer some help as his parking skills were now so well practised. With a closer look, he realised the driver was Apricot and Maureen was sitting in the passenger seat. Now he had to go and help.

'We wanted to surprise you!' shrieked Apricot.

'Surprise? You two are enough to give me a heart attack,' Frank said. 'Did you bring Mirabelle?'

'She declined. I'm overnighting with Maureen and Plum didn't want to stay away from home,' Apricot said.

Maureen looked puzzled.

'Well, let's get the wheelchair out and get you comfortable,' Frank said. 'There'll be space along the front row.'

The choir's leader rushed past as they entered the main hall and Frank saw Apricot's head turn. The leader, who was also the conductor, had already changed and looked dapper in a black cotton shirt. He was straightening his orange necktie. A group of choir women drifted through the hall, again wearing black tops, enhanced by draped orange scarves.

'They all look like Sarah Bernhardt with their flowing silk neckwear,' Apricot commented, rather too loudly.

'I need to go and get changed too,' Frank said. 'Will you be all right here? The loos are over there and here's a programme for you. I'll see you at the end, it's only an hour and a half.'

He rushed off but couldn't resist peeping back to see if Maureen was okay. She and Apricot were chatting and smiling. Frank looked up Sarah Bernhardt on his phone before changing his shirt.

They looked nothing like her.

The performance went well. Their conductor had a smooth tongue and warmed the audience up with stories about each piece of music, making it an entertaining evening for all. Frank was self-conscious at first but quickly forgot to focus on his special guests and relaxed, opening his lungs enthusiastically. The guy on percussion dropped his cymbal in the next to last song and the audience burst out laughing before the conductor asked them to join in the final song, a stirring rendition of "Can You Feel the Love Tonight".

'Oh, that was lovely, Frank, I'm so proud,' Maureen told him when he returned front of house.

'It's such a shame Plum missed it,' Apricot said and Maureen once again looked bewildered.

'She means Mirabelle,' Frank laughed. 'Apricot will explain later.'

'What's your conductor called? I must go and congratulate him,' Apricot said and moved towards the man before Frank could even answer.

'Is he single?' Maureen asked.

'Recently divorced,' Frank said.

'Oh dear, perhaps you should rescue him,' Maureen chuckled.

'No this could be fun, let's leave them to it. Would you like a drink from the bar?'

'A sparkling water would be very nice.'

When Frank returned with two glasses of water, Apricot and the conductor had disappeared.

'I do hope I've not lost my lift home,' Maureen said, just as one of the sopranos approached Frank.

'Hi, Olga, can I introduce my mother, Maureen? She lives not far away in Lowestoft.'

'That's nice,' Olga said. 'You have a fine son.'

'I do indeed,' Maureen replied. 'I loved your solo, Olga, you have a splendid voice.'

'Thank you so much,' Olga's ample bosom lifted worryingly. 'I teach music and singing at Felixstowe Academy.'

'How splendid,' Maureen said.

'I wish all my students there were as keen to learn as Frank. I've been helping him out with his technique, along with our leader, of course. Frank's made wonderful progress – could go far. I'd love to give him some private lessons.'

Olga edged closer, *too close for comfort.*

'We need to hit the road soon. I'm taking Olga, and Sharon, that's her over there,' he pointed, 'I'm giving them both a lift home and we have further to travel than you. Now where is Apricot?'

'Oh, I get it, you mean the woman with apricot coloured hair.' Olga laughed. 'She's out at the back with our esteemed leader. He's looking a bit trapped, actually.' She pouted and winked provocatively at Frank.

'I'll go and get her,' Frank said, hoping it was safe to leave Olga alone with Maureen.

Olga could be almost as overpowering as Apricot and he didn't want her giving Maureen any funny ideas about their friendship. He was relieved Sharon would be in the car too on the way home. He liked Sharon and it amused him to think such a warm and vibrant voice could come from a sparrow of a woman like her. At least both would be in the car tonight and again on the way to Norwich. Sharon would make a good chaperone.

Frank found Apricot leaning in close to the conductor and paused to see what would happen next. The harassed man looked tired and took a step back. *He'll be as ready for a summer break as me once these concerts are over*, Frank thought. He knew despite the rest, he'd miss the social contact he enjoyed with the choir. What if he left Felixstowe for good? *How dull would life be without the amusing attentions of Mrs Olga Smit and the chirping of the sweet little sparrow?*

What is it with these women, he thought? At least Apricot doesn't flirt or make me feel uncomfortable like Olga. Her looks and comments had been a game at first, until this week when they started to worry him. He remembered Mirabelle's comment many weeks ago now about not letting his blue eyes stray. Was he slightly tempted? He tried to tell himself not, when the voice boomed in his head.

Drop the soprano home first just in case. Let the sparrow be your protection.

The women were very quiet on the drive back to Felixstowe. *I guess we're all a bit worn out,* Frank thought. He wondered what Mirabelle was up to, and whether it would be too late to phone her once he got home. Their phone calls had been brief and unsatisfactory of late. He tried not to ask too much about Andy and Mirabelle seemed to have lost interest in anything Frank was up to. They hadn't talked any more about him moving in and she hadn't said she loved him for a while now but then again, he hadn't said it to her. He had thought he might stay with her on the way back from Norwich but now he was giving lifts to Olga and Sharon, that wouldn't work. At least they appreciated him and liked his singing, and so did his mother. Mirabelle hadn't even tried to come to a concert. He wondered if she would bother to come to Felixstowe with Apricot for the Book Festival at the end of next month. They needed to book their places and somewhere to stay if they were actually coming.

'Olga, will you and Mr Smit be going to any of the Book Festival in June?' he asked out of the blue. 'I'm hoping Mirabelle, my partner, will be coming with Apricot, her friend you've just met.'

'I see,' Olga said. 'Well, I might go to some events but my husband doesn't really do things like that. He's not the most sociable, I'm afraid.'

'Oh dear,' Sharon chirped, 'I'll be going to lots. I loved it last year. Why don't you come with me Olga?'

'I… er… maybe, I'll have to check my diary.'

'I was wondering if either of you could recommend a nice B and B where Mirabelle and Apricot could stay?' Frank asked.

'Can't they stay with you?' Olga said.

'I don't really have room for two ladies. My place is very small.'

'Really, oh dear, what a shame,' Olga said.

'I know a couple of places. I'll jot down some names for you when you get to my house,' Sharon said. 'I hope I'm not taking you out of your way?'

'Not a problem, Sharon,' Frank replied.

Olga remained quiet.

'I'll pick you ladies up for Norwich around three o'clock as planned. Don't forget your scarves,' Frank said when he dropped Olga off. 'I'll collect Sharon first and then come round for you, Olga.

CHAPTER 34

That night, after a dinner to celebrate the final concert, and back at the Premier Inn in Norwich, Sharon kissed Frank goodnight, so fully on the lips that he didn't know what had hit him. It was thrilling but worrying, even slightly terrifying. He had trouble getting to sleep.

The next morning, he breakfasted early, wondering if she might join him. *No such luck.* When he drove them home, he managed to be calm and clear headed while both the ladies were quietly hung over. It made for a pleasant journey. He drove smoothly, appreciating the lack of small talk which had been exhausting the night before when he sat with them over dinner.

When he got home, having dropped them off in turn, Frank thought again about the kiss. It probably meant nothing to Sharon, which was a good thing, even so he couldn't deny it had happened. Sharon had made no reference to it when he dropped her off, just gave him a soft peck to thank him for the lift. He wasn't sure if he was relieved or not.

Like a sparrow.

Frank pottered about and delayed phoning Mirabelle although he knew he should. He reimagined last night's kiss which had made him feel confused and now he couldn't settle.

Having known Mirabelle for just nine months was he already stuck in a rut? There might be another world out there for him to explore while he was still able. The new confidence Mirabelle had given him was wonderful but maybe her job was now done and it was time for him to be a mature, independent man, not the skulking, inhibited bloke he'd been for most of his life. He had thought he was willing to share his new life and his money with Mirabelle and she'd obviously been of the same mindset but then along came Andy. Frank wouldn't choose to share his future and his inheritance with that wastrel but if he really loved Mirabelle would that matter? Could he make it work?

His mobile rang and it was her. He let it go to voice mail and went to make a cup of tea. He then felt guilty and phoned her back.

'Sorry I missed your call. I need to come and see you,' he said.

'Oh, is everything all right? I just wanted to know how the concerts went. Are you glad it's all over?'

'I'm okay, just tired I suppose. It was fun. I'm planning to drive over to see you tomorrow and we can talk properly.'

'That'll be lovely. You do sound a bit wiped out,'

'I'll have a quiet day to catch up and then tomorrow I'll be fine.'

'Good, Andy will be out with his new friend so we'll have the place to ourselves. It seems ages since we've really talked.'

'I'm not sure if I'll be staying over or not. It depends. I might want to see Maureen the next day.'

'You only saw her on Wednesday and according to Apricot, you all had a lovely time. You seem to want to spend more time with her than with me,' Mirabelle commented.

'A bit like you and Andy, then?'

As soon as the words came out of his mouth Frank knew he'd messed up.

'That's ridiculous. I don't know how long I'll have him for, I have to make the most of it.'

'And I could say the same about my mother,' Frank replied.

'Now you've made us both sound like stupid teenagers. I'll see you in time for lunch tomorrow and we'll talk,' and with that she put the phone down.

The next morning, after another damaged night, Frank packed his overnight bag, wondering whether or not he'd need it. Actually, he might not even go to see Maureen until after his next series of night shifts, so why had he mentioned her to Mirabelle? He drove more aggressively than usual and at one point sped through an amber light as it turned to red. Normally, he'd most certainly have stopped. His heart fluttered and he looked in his rear-view mirror, checking for traffic cameras or a police car. His licence was much too precious to be taken away so soon and he really loved having a car. He slowed down and tried to breathe calmly in preparation for what might be a difficult conversation in Ipswich.

Andy was just leaving as he arrived at Mirabelle's door.

'Hi, Frank, have a nice lunch. Ma's got some paddle fish in for you.' Andy smiled or was it a smirk?

'He's in a better mood and looking smart,' Frank commented, deciding to be positive for Mirabelle's sake as she came to the door.

'In you come.' She pecked him on the cheek, definitely more a pigeon's peck than a sparrow's. 'I think it's a date but he hasn't let on. He's meeting someone he got together with on last Sunday's Park Run.'

Perhaps if he's feeling better, he'll drink less and be more civil and things could be all right after all, Frank thought. The kitchen smelt of freshly baked bread and filter coffee and he wondered if he was mad to lose all this.

'Tell me all about the concerts over coffee before I get the lunch on. It is good to see you, Frank.'

She leaned in for a proper kiss, parting her lips. Frank felt awkward when he reciprocated. Mirabelle didn't seem to notice he was putting on a performance.

'I'm sorry I missed Bungay. I had a dental appointment early the next morning and no way could have stayed the night.'

'Apricot didn't tell me that, she made it sound as if you didn't want to come.'

'For goodness' sake, of course I wanted to come but I'd lost a filling and I daren't put the dentist off.'

'Tooth okay now?' Frank asked and she replied with a wide smile.

The day continued with chat and food and a

late afternoon walk felt almost normal, but not quite.

'No one cooks paddle fish quite like you, Mirabelle,' Frank commented as they walked past a fish and chip shop.

'And nobody washes up like you Frank,' she replied.

'Is that all I'm good for?' Frank said.

'What do you want, a list?'

They were watching television that evening when Andy came home, so drunk he couldn't find the keyhole in the front door. Frank let him in.

'Still hanging around?' Andy slurred. 'The old dear hasn't booted you out yet then?'

'And somehow you've managed to keep her onside too. Miracles never cease. Had a good day?'

'Bloody marvellous. Where's Mum?'

'Putting her feet up in the front room,' Frank said.

'Hope I haven't interrupted anything?' Andy sneered and gave Frank a shove as he walked into the sitting room. Frank felt like delivering him a right hook. He hadn't struck out in anger in all the years he'd been sober and didn't like the feeling that swept over him. He went to the bathroom to cool down and brush his teeth to quash the desire for a smoke. Frank returned to find mother and son sprawled at either end the sofa. Andy was swigging from a can of lager, while Mirabelle was quizzing him about his date.

Frank sat in an armchair and listened to

Andy's tale about the bloke called Mel who had no end of business interests and was going to help him get a job.

Frank literally had to bite his tongue to stop himself asking if Mel employed drunks but when Andy got up for another lager, he couldn't stop himself

'Haven't you had enough Andy? How about a coffee?'

'Who are you to talk? I've heard all about you, I know you're an alcoholic and just because you've come into some moolah, you think you're top of the pile.'

'Stop it, Andy. I told you that in confidence, just to explain things a bit,' Mirabelle said. 'I'm so sorry, Frank.'

'What things needed explaining?' Frank snarled. 'Recovering alcoholic, yes. Sober for nearly twenty years, absolutely, so don't talk to me like that, Andy. And whilst we're talking straight, don't take advantage of your mother's good nature. I hope you're paying your way in this house or at least helping her out a bit.'

'Good nature, my foot. It's your money she's after. I haven't anything to give her.'

'Stop it, Andy. You're drunk and out of control. We'll talk again when you've calmed down. Don't listen to him, Frank,' Mirabelle pleaded.

'I think you need help,' Frank said, taking a few deep breaths. 'I can put you in touch with some organisations.'

'Bugger off,' Andy said and stormed out of the room, crashing into the easel as he went.

Mirabelle looked on the verge of tears and as Frank went to put an arm round her, she flinched.

'He hasn't hurt you, has he?'

'Of course not. I've tried to help him, Frank and some days he's better than others. I've already fallen out with Apricot over him, I can't fall out with you too. I need you,' she sobbed.

'You need to be firm with him.'

'But you can see what he's like. It only makes him more difficult if I'm firm.'

'Like I am, you mean?'

'Yes, and Apricot too, she tried when she came round. She's not been back since.'

'He needs to speak to someone, maybe that nice GP of yours?'

'I don't think he'll go. I thought this new chap, Mel, might help but I was obviously wrong there. I don't know what to do. I think I've been in denial about how bad this is.'

'Could you contact his father?'

'It's crossed my mind but he lives back in Wales now. Perhaps I should try to make contact. I suppose I can get an address from his cousin. Let's go to bed, Frank. You are staying tonight, aren't you?'

'Yes, I'll stay,' Frank said. He thought a sympathetic cuddle was in order. He really wasn't in the mood for anything more and by the looks of her nor was she.

Over breakfast the next day when Andy was still in bed, Frank and Mirabelle ate scrambled eggs on toast and skirted around the subject that had caused them both to toss and turn in the night, stealing the duvet from one another.'

'Let's talk about Andy and the options,' Frank said bluntly. 'Give him an ultimatum, tell him to leave unless he agrees to see the GP or else let him be and you go and stay elsewhere for a short break, maybe with Apricot.'

'I can't abandon him and anyway I daren't leave him alone in my house, he'd wreck it. Apricot wouldn't want me anyway. Could I stay with you for a few days?'

'You know there's no room and the landlady wouldn't like it.'

'Could you come and stay here a bit more?'

'Even though I've reduced my hours, I'm still working and I'm afraid I seem to stir the boy up more than help. Involving his father and getting him some treatment might be the best thing.'

'I didn't think you meant it before but you don't want to come here to stay do you?' she asked. 'I really thought you'd have handed in your notice and moved in by now. What's happening, Frank?'

'It doesn't feel right yet. It'll be a big step.'

'It's not just Andy, is it?'

'He's the main reason but there are other things too, I might actually miss Felixstowe and work. Retiring will make me feel old and then there's the choir.'

'I see,' she said quietly. 'You mean you'll miss your independence.'

'It might just be a coincidence but things just don't feel the same between us since Andy.

274

I want to be supportive but sorry, I can't move in at the moment.'

'Perhaps we should leave it at that and take a break. I don't want your grudging support if you're having doubts. I thought you loved me.'

'I thought I did too,' Frank mumbled.

'I think you should go.'

'What now?'

'Yes, that's right. Go visit your mother,' she said with a new bitterness in her voice

'Don't be like that, will you be safe?' Frank asked.

'No need to pretend, Frank. Might have known you had no staying power'

'That's unfair, how about your part in this, telling me what I can and can't do,' Frank raised his voice.

'Don't be a baby, I have one child to look after already, I don't need another!' she yelled.

'Charming, you don't need me, then?' Frank replied.

'I've survived on my own for much of my adult life, so I'll survive now,' she announced. 'You go to Mummy. Take care of yourself, Frank. Goodbye.'

Frank stormed out of the kitchen and upstairs. He threw his things into his trusty holdall and on the way across the landing, looked at the picture of Ricky on the landing with distaste.

Never did like cats, did you?

Mirabelle was nowhere to be seen when Frank stomped downstairs and out through the front door. He drove away and stopped in a lay-by up the road to phone his mother.

'Hi Mum, thought I'd pop up and spend some time with you. Are you free?'

CHAPTER 35

He picked up some cod and chips on the way to Maureen's, knowing she'd worry about feeding him at short notice. She usually just had a tin of soup for her lunch and that wouldn't be enough to satisfy Frank today, he needed some real comfort food, accompanied by white bread and butter and tomato ketchup. Surely she'd have ketchup in the cupboard?

They ate quickly while it was still warm. The cod was fresh and succulent, almost as good as Mirabelle's paddle fish.

'This is grand, Frank, what a lovely surprise. Now, what's up? You usually give me more notice,' Maureen asked.

'Nothing really, I just saw an opportunity and took it. I thought we could look at the garden and make some plans now the weather's improving,' he said.

'That would be good but I thought your ladies were going to be in on that.'

Frank smirked when she said "your ladies" as if he had a harem.

'I suppose I should tell you Mirabelle and I are taking a break.'

'For goodness' sake... I mean oh dear, I'm sorry to hear that. But really, that modern phrase rather annoys me. Either you're together or you're not, stay together or spilt up, why delay the inevitable? Goodness me, I sound as crotchety as Della. This knee's bothering me, I'll take a painkiller after lunch.'

'I know what you mean but life's not always so simple. I don't really want to go into the details, I came here for a distraction and to talk about you. Are you fit for a drive to the garden centre this afternoon if we take the folding wheelchair?'

Frank enjoyed drawing up a simple plan of the garden and working out which areas had most of the day's sun and which had shade. They talked about favourite flowers and colours and Frank made suggestions about plants he'd come to know while working with Reg. Maureen seemed to value the connection.

On the drive to the garden centre, Frank asked what she really thought about Della.

'She's always been a tricky one and I know life has dealt her a few hard blows but she's been worse and more irascible since Reg's funeral.'

'That stupid will is never going to make life easy between the two sides of the family. I should never have accepted the money. It's caused way too much grief,' Frank said.

'It's not your fault and it's not about sides, we're all one family now. Yes, the will floored Della and Gus but look what it's done for you and me. Without it, we might not have found each other. And apart from this recent problem with Mirabelle, your life has improved no end. I'm sure it's just a blip.'

'Who knows? But meanwhile, I am trying to do the right thing by the Halls. Gus has started to accept me, and my contributions, but Della is another story.'

'As I say, she's always been the one in charge. She loved her status as long-term housekeeper in that big house, bossed poor Reg around something awful and cow-towed to old Arthur Trelawney. She's lost her status and her health as well as her husband. She's okay for money, though, so don't fret too much about that. I know for a fact Arthur saw her right.'

'How come you know that?'

'Reg wasn't as daft as everyone made out, not until the last lap anyhow. He told me quite a bit about his relationship with Della and hers with Arthur, that's why I wasn't as surprised as some about the will.'

'I can accept that's one reason for the dramatic upset but I don't understand why Gus was left out?'

'He did tend to side with his mother and talk down to Reg. He used to call his dad a country bumpkin.'

'He was a bit,' Frank said.

'With hidden depths,' Maureen added with a little grin. 'Actually, I thought Della would pick herself up after Reg had gone, especially if and when Gus made her a grandmother. Waiting for that alongside her own health problems has made things worse than they might have been.'

'There's hope yet then. Sandra and Gus are having more treatment and another large bill has been paid from the account to their private hospital.'

'There's always hope, Frank. I just hope Della's fit enough to enjoy a grandchild when it arrives.'

'Here we are. It's busy but I can park over there. Did you bring your disabled badge?'

'Yes, but I hate that word. I'm not disabled, I'm just not very mobile,' Maureen said.

'If you say so. Now pass me the badge and I'll get the wheelchair out, unless you'd rather walk,' he teased.

As he pushed her round the paths, Maureen ticked off the plants she wanted from her list.

'Perhaps we should have asked Gus's advice or is it too late?' she asked. 'He's the expert these days.'

'He's got his hands full at the moment. Don't you trust me?'

'Yes, course I do. I was just thinking,' Maureen said.

'Me too. I could offer to pay for Della to see someone privately about her pancreas?' Frank asked.

'Nice thought. I did mention something along those lines to Gus last time we spoke but apparently, she's already got an appointment to see a top man at Addenbrookes on the NHS. I think it would only complicate things.'

'If you say so,' Frank said, looking at a nice standard bay tree in a pot. 'This would look good by your front door.'

'Maybe,' Maureen said. 'Frank, you do know you can't pay for everything and solve everyone's problems, don't you? Guilt about the will won't be solved like that, it'll be solved by communication.'

'I guess so but I can help a bit. I wondered about you going private for your other hip replacement.'

'That's very kind but no thanks, I'd rather stay with my familiar team. It's not just the consultant you see, it's the whole team, specialist nurses, physios and occupational therapists, you get them all if you're in the system. It helps that they know me already. Change systems and the communication goes haywire so you can literally fall between two stools.'

'I'm pleased you still have faith in the NHS. Are you sure you're not stalling on this next hip replacement, delaying the inevitable?' Frank asked.

'Touché,' Maureen chuckled, 'and actually it's the knee next. I knew you weren't listening. I have to have this knee done before the next hip if I survive. They say knees are harder to get over than hips.'

They took their plant list to the order desk and after some discussion, arranged a convenient delivery date for the selected plants and shrubs.

Back at the bungalow, Maureen needed a lie down. Frank made her a cup of tea and gave her some more painkillers before setting off back to Felixstowe.

He drove more carefully than before. He thought of Mirabelle and how they'd progressed too quickly with their relationship and made rash plans, despite his gut telling him to take it slowly. He still couldn't help thinking she'd have really enjoyed the outing to the plant nursery. He wondered if he'd manage the planting on his own when he returned? Of course he would.

At home he checked his phone and for a brief moment thought the message posted there might be from Sharon, but of course it was Gus, whose number he recognised once he put his glasses on.

Gus's text message said Della had been admitted urgently to Addenbrookes with yet another pancreatic flare up. He hadn't told Maureen yet and wouldn't do so until they knew more, maybe tomorrow.

What am I supposed to do now? Frank thought.

He texted Maureen to say he was home safely without even mentioning Della and texted Gus to say sorry, asking to be kept informed. He suggested they might have another meeting when the time felt right. For some reason, after that, Frank had an urge to tell Mirabelle about Della but knew tonight he couldn't.

CHAPTER 36

Frank was back to his old routine of "work, eat, sleep" with an occasional phone call to his mother thrown in. Mirabelle hadn't phoned him to make the first move, so he held back from calling her. He wondered more than once whether to phone Sharon but thought better of it. Going for mystery drives on his days off gave him more pleasure than anything nowadays. He drove around and explored the Suffolk villages and towns. One day, aiming for Eastland, which he still had trouble finding and the satnav didn't help much with that either, he must have taken a wrong turn and found himself on the outskirts of Stowmarket.

Frank parked in the town centre and took a walk. He visited the church and the shops and had a snack at a sandwich bar. He came upon a park and went to check out the planted beds. Children were running about and playing with their parents after school. He'd never had that privilege and wanted to watch the children having fun but knew he mustn't stare and risk getting challenged.

He walked away from the play area to view a border of lavender and aster and heard a woman's voice call out. A little chap in a blue anorak rushed past him towards the swings.

'Jacob, slow down. Wait for Mabel,' came the same woman's voice more clearly.

A little girl ran after the boy. The girl tripped, lay on the floor and screamed as the woman caught up and scooped her up into her arms.

'Jacob! Do as you're told and come back here now!' The woman sounded tired as she rubbed the girl's knee. 'No harm done, nothing a nice swing won't cure.'

The crying stopped and the woman, presumably the mother, Frank thought, kissed the top of the little girl's head.

'Jacob, please hold her hand and go slowly to the swings. You know your sister can't keep up with you.'

Jacob sweetly took the girl's hand and looked up at Frank as he walked past. Frank couldn't help but smile.

'Hello, I know you,' Jacob said.

The woman pulled him away.

'How many times must I tell you not to talk to strangers?' she said sharply.

'It's him, the nice man from the café.'

'Don't be silly, Jacob. Come away now and help Mabel onto the small swing.'

The little boy put his head down and crossed his arms. The woman stood and waited patiently until he looked up. He suddenly yelled, 'Daddy, look Daddy's coming.'

'Hurrah for that, about time,' sighed the woman.

Frank recognised Max in his running gear, jogging towards the little family.

'Sorry love, I got carried away and ran further than planned.' He held out his smart phone to the woman. 'Look, 7K on Strava.'

Frank hesitated, should he interrupt the family outing? Why not?

'Hi! Max, isn't it?' he said staying back at a sensible distance.

'Frank, is that you?' Max grinned.

'It's me all right. I just wanted to say hello and ask how you're all doing.'

'We're fine thanks. This is Jenny, my wife. Jenny this is Frank who helped find Jacob that day in Ipswich,' he said.

'I thought so, pleased to meet you. I'm glad the children are all right.'

'Tired after a day at school and nursery but fine thanks. I suppose I should say thank you for what you did that day. I'm sorry I've not had chance sooner.'

'You've nothing to apologise for, I can see you have your hands full. Great kids.'

'What brings you here?' Max asked.

'I had a day off and took my new car out for a drive. It brought me here by accident. I was exploring the area around Eastland and got rather lost. I've not been out this way since the funeral.'

'Oh, the funeral,' Max said.

There was an awkward silence. Jenny shuffled her feet.

'Where are you living now? I heard you might move to Ipswich,' Max asked.

'That's on hold at the moment. I'm still in Felixstowe,' Frank replied light-heartedly.

Jacob, who'd been pushing Mabel on the swing, came over to the grown-ups.

'I'll go,' Jenny said and replaced her son supervising Mabel.

Max and Frank drifted closer.

'Hello again,' Jacob said. 'I told her it was you.'

'Hello, young man, how are you?' Frank asked. He'd have liked to do a high five but thought that might be a bit too familiar.

'Very well, thank you,' Jacob said politely. 'Uncle Gus said you're alright really.'

'Did he now? Well, I'm pleased to hear it,' Frank smiled.

'That'll do Jacob. Go and have a go on the balancing board and we'll follow.'

'Gus told us you'd met up a few times and that you've found your mother now.'

'The last few months have been full-on. I've been trying to do the right thing by the Hall family, perhaps I should now say my family? We're getting there.'

'It's been tough on them all. Della talks to Jenny quite often so we've heard her side of the story. The old girl's still pretty bitter but she's been almost too ill to think about it lately.'

'Is it that bad? Mum hasn't said anything and Gus hasn't told me much.'

'Gus isn't telling Maureen so as not to upset her but Della has had another major surgery and still isn't out of the woods. I think you should phone Gus if you want details.'

'Perhaps I'd better.'

'Look, I think we need to get these two back for tea. Good to see you. Can you find your way home?' Max laughed but it was a kind laugh, not sarcastic like Gus might have been.

Frank waved goodbye to the kids, feeling

pleased to see Jacob again and in good form. It was nice to be introduced to the boy's mother. The unexpected meeting brought thoughts of Tricia to his mind as he walked to the car. His lonely day of random wandering had turned out better than expected. He turned on the car radio, set the satnav and sang along with the songs playing on the tea-time programme as he set off for home. It was only when Dylan came on singing "Mr Tambourine Man" that he missed Mirabelle.

He stopped at a petrol station to fill up in preparation for an early get-away for Lowestoft the next day. He browsed through the magazines near the checkout and picked up a gardening magazine to entertain him that evening. He'd finished the books he'd borrowed but before settling down with the magazine, he wanted to phone Gus to be put in the picture about Della.

Maybe give him a nudge and ask about the redhead too.

CHAPTER 37

Gus dithered when Frank asked him how much he could tell Maureen, saying he wasn't sure.

'She's bound to ask if I've spoken to you. Does she even know Della's in hospital?'

'Doubt it, I haven't said anything about it,' Gus replied.

'I thought not. Someone's got to tell her.'

'You can, it's better face-to-face than on the phone,' Gus said.

'Maureen's not as fragile as you make out, I'm sure she'll be fine if I just tell her straight that Della's had further surgery,' Frank said.

'You can't just come out with it - you'll have to build up to it gently.'

'I can do gently but you haven't told me much. How serious is it? I'm sorry to have to ask but might she die?'

Frank heard Gus gulp down the phone and wondered if he'd been too blunt.

'Listen, she's in Intensive Care and they say the next 48 hours are critical,' Gus choked away a cough. 'I'm here on the unit now. They've given me a room I can use overnight.'

'Oh, I see, I'm sorry. Is Sandra with you?'

'No, she's resting.'

'I hope she's not ill too?'

'No.'

Silence followed.

'Can I do anything to help?'

'No. I've got to go now. You do your thing with Maureen and I'll phone you when I know more.'

Frank knew now was not the time to ask about Tricia. Perhaps he needed to forget about the redhead who kept popping up in his thoughts. As it was, he was left feeling he'd not handled the situation well. If he'd known Della's situation was quite so serious, he'd have made a better job of it. He made a cup of tea and opened his magazine but couldn't concentrate on the words so just looked at the pictures. He wasn't over-fond of Della but he felt strangely affected by what Gus had said. Poor guy, he thought, it's not long since he buried his dad. Frank got out his road map to check how far Cambridge was from Ipswich and was surprised to see it was about as far as Lowestoft but in the opposite direction.

On his drive to Lowestoft the next morning, he rehearsed what he would say to Maureen then thought about what he had to do in the garden. The delivery van was unloading trays of plants as he parked the car. Maureen was leaning on her walking frame, directing proceedings. Her face lit up when she saw Frank.

'Look at this lovely lot,' she said happily. 'It's a good job we added compost and soil improver to our list.'

'How are you, Mum?' Frank asked.

'Tip top. I'll see the delivery man off and then I can show you where I want things to go,' she replied.

'Have you taken too many tablets or

something?'

'No, why? Aren't I allowed to be excited about my new garden?' she said.

'Of course you are. You just seem a bit hyper that's all.'

'Rubbish. I do have some new tablets from the doctor but I've also had a letter from the hospital with a date for my new knee. Isn't that good?'

'Great. You're happy then, I get it. Give me the date when we go inside, then I'll change into my scruff gear and we'll make a start. You know I can only stay the one night, don't you?'

'That's fine. I thought while the weather's nice you could bring my chair out. I'll sit and give orders while you work. Get yourself a cool drink first.'

Frank decided not to delay the news about Della, it would seem odd to just come out with it later in the day. Maureen was remarkably chilled about it, probably due to her own elevated state. She made all the right noises but didn't seem at all upset but then again, they weren't particularly close. He'd been trying to play happy families with the Halls but perhaps he'd created a false image of his relatives. He should have known better - life wasn't a fairy tale - it could be shit or just plain ordinary.

After a hard day's digging and a nice meal from the freezer, pre-cooked by Cathy, whom Maureen described as a gem, they both flopped down in the easy chairs. Frank double-checked the date of Maureen's operation and realised the only other thing in his diary around that time was the Felixstowe Book Festival. He reminded Maureen that Apricot was going to send her a virtual link for some of the talks being recorded.

'She's already set it up for me but I can't access it until the festival starts. Apricot's paid a nice donation and booked the sessions I'm interested in. Can you take her this envelope? I need to pay her back, I don't like owing,' Maureen said.

'I won't be going to Ipswich for a while, I told you Mirabelle and me were having a break,' Frank replied, trying to sound nonchalant.

'Oh, for goodness' sake, haven't you sorted that out yet? Do you miss her?'

'A bit, but things changed. I don't want to go into it right now.'

'Fair enough but women like that don't grow on trees at your age.'

Frank tried to ignore the voice, *Plums grow on trees!*

'Why are you rubbing the back of your head, have you pulled a neck muscle?'

'Maybe but I'm okay' Frank said.

'Do you want one of my new painkillers?'

'No, I can't. Not very wise taking someone else's pills anyway. I'll go to bed soon but first, talk me through the operation. Presumably you'll need extra help afterwards?'

'I'm planning to go to a rehab unit for 2 weeks initially, then I'll get Cathy to do some extra days.'

'I could take some time off,' Frank offered.

291

'We'll see. I think I can sort it, dear, but it's kind of you to offer.'

Thankfully Frank got the garden tidied up the next day before a light drizzle arrived to help the plants settle in. Perfect timing, Maureen said. She hobbled out to see him off and announced the new tablets were so good she might postpone the operation.

Frank jumped at her in despair. 'You might go to the back of the list, or not get recalled until mid-winter. Just get it over with while the weather is nice and you're in good form.'

'Do you think so?'

'Yes. It'll make the recovery easier and actually I'm not sure about these miracle tablets, I looked at the advice leaflet and it says short courses only, risk of addiction.'

'I don't read those leaflets - they frighten you to death.'

'Mum!' Frank exclaimed. 'And here's me thinking you're an intelligent woman. Imagine if you had a fall while you're waiting. I'm sure Mirabelle would say get it done.'

'Would she now?' Maureen raised an eyebrow. 'I'll soon be cutting down on the tablets. Get yourself off and don't worry. I won't really postpone it and I'll keep you informed. Don't forget to give Apricot that envelope when you eventually see her.'

Frank phoned Apricot about the money when he got home and to see if she'd booked her tickets for the Book Festival. She was as organised as ever and had a room booked at a nice B and B, so as to make a little holiday of it.

'Are you coming alone?' Frank asked.

'I am, why do you ask?'

'Why do you think?' Frank replied.

'Yes, well, it'll just be me, do you mind? How about you?'

'I'm good. There's a possibility I might go to a couple of the events with a local friend,' he lied, 'but perhaps I could meet you for a meal one evening.'

'Thank you, Frank, that would be lovely. I'll let you arrange that. The Saturday night would suit me best, let me know where and when to meet you. Just one thing, I'm not fond of Indian food.'

Frank smiled when he put down the phone, Apricot was certainly particular. While he was in the mood, he had an impulse to phone Sharon and ask if she wanted to meet him sometime soon. He had nothing on after work and if things went well, he could maybe accompany her to a book event. It would impress his mother if nothing else and it might stop her going on about Mirabelle. He felt very brave as he punched Sharon's number into the phone, holding his breath until she answered.

CHAPTER 38

Frank and Sharon went out on a few dates after that phone call. They enjoyed some evening meals and even went to the cinema. He liked her company and she let him put his arm round her shoulder in the cinema. Frank waited for a spark to ignite at the end of each outing but she only wanted a lift home and a fleeting kiss. As it happened, he was happy enough with that and wondered what the deeper and more meaningful kiss that took place in Norwich was all about. Was it all in his imagination?

Sharon invited him to a talk at the library on the Saturday morning of the festival. It was about the Felixstowe Ferry and she thought he'd be interested to hear about it. Frank knew Apricot's schedule and she'd be at a workshop elsewhere so he thought it would be safe to go. He didn't know why but he didn't want Apricot taking tales back to Ipswich. He'd already factored in that he'd have more control over the conversation at dinner than if they just bumped into each other at random.

Frank felt quite nervous when the festival weekend arrived. Had he taken too much on? His friend Bill had teased him all week about dating two women in one weekend, even offered to take one off his hands. Frank almost took him up on it and was starting to wish he had. Sharon was late arriving for coffee before the ferry talk so Frank read a newspaper left on his table and watched the customers drift in and out. *Oh good*, he thought, *she's stood me up, I can go home.* Then Sharon arrived and he couldn't believe the sight. Her wavy, mousey brown hair had been dyed to a gingery-red colour and styled so curls fell onto the shoulders of her dark green, almost black jacket. She walked awkwardly in high heeled shoes.

'Goodness, hello,' was all Frank managed to say.

'What do you think?' she asked.

'Erm...very nice, I think. When did this happen?'

'You don't like it? Oh God, I've made a mistake. I thought it'd make me more exciting.' She looked upset.

'No, it's fine, I mean you were fine as you were. You just reminded me of someone else and it's rather taken me by surprise.'

'An ex-girlfriend I expect?' Sharon queried.

'No, nothing like that, just a woman I once crossed paths with but you're really nothing like her. Let me get you a coffee, we still have twenty minutes.'

Sharon seemed calmer when Frank returned with the coffees and they exchanged small-talk until it was time to walk to the venue of the talk. Frank listened intently, finding the subject matter most interesting while Sharon shuffled and twitched and looked as if she might take off any minute.

Once a sparrow, always a sparrow.

You can't pretend to be something you are not, Frank thought. *It's a bit like, once a dockworker always a dockworker. The choir has made us both feel we can briefly be someone else but does it last?*

After the lecture, Sharon excused herself and rushed away. She said she'd phone but he had a feeling she wouldn't. She didn't exactly take flight, more like tottered off down the high street at a pace. The thought of following her only lasted a second and he turned away and walked slowly to the promenade. He passed the Martello Tower and aimed for Landguard Fort. It was a long walk but one he often enjoyed on a day off. He looked over to the docks, as always marvelling at the rows of giant cranes and the stacked containers that towered over the buildings where he worked. He wondered how much longer he'd be there. Technology had taken over many of the jobs he used to do and he was almost ready to leave but not quite there yet. He'd known nothing else for years and when he did go, it would be a big step.

When he returned home, he put his feet up, preparing himself for his next date. At least Apricot would have no expectations and he wouldn't have to make too much effort because she would do all the talking. He dressed smartly and put Maureen's envelope in his top pocket. They arrived at the Italian restaurant at the same time and were shown to their table.

'Perfect,' Apricot said, as the waiter held her chair. 'Nice place and you look very smart Frank.'

Frank lowered his shoulders and

straightened his new shirt so it lay well across his broad chest beneath his jacket. It was unusual for him to wear a white shirt and this was a trial run.

'You look very nice yourself, Apricot, have you had a good couple of days?' Frank asked.

'Thank you. Do you know, it's been lovely?' Apricot said. 'The B and B is charming and I've met some lovely people at the talks.'

She went on to tell him about the sessions she'd attended in great detail, then announced, 'It's a nicer town than I expected.'

'You said that about Lowestoft when you first went there,' Frank laughed.

'I'm easier to please than people think,' Apricot said dryly.

'Let's order. Have whatever you want, it's my treat,' Frank said.

'That's very kind. I don't often get treated by a gentleman,' she said, without a hint of flirting.

'And I don't often get called a gentleman,' Frank replied in a similar tone.

He longed to ask her if she'd seen the choirmaster again but thought better of it, guessing she'd have told him by now if she had. She ordered a large glass of dry white wine while Frank had a bottle of sparkling water to wash down a sharing plate of antipasti. Each chose a different pasta dish for their main course.

'I do admire how you've handled your addiction,' Apricot announced during the meal.

Frank was unused to such directness and

hesitated before replying. 'It's Reg I have to thank for that.'

'You must have made quite an impression on each other that summer.'

'Yep, something just clicked between us. At the time, he just needed a companion, I needed a mentor and it worked.'

'It's a great story.'

'A good beginning but it came to an untidy end, didn't it? Still, the messy stuff is beginning to sort itself out,' Frank said.

'Let's hope so, for your mother's sake if nothing else. I've grown rather fond of dear Maureen. We phone each other regularly you know.'

'I'm pleased. You seem to have a lot in common, your mutual love of books for a start.'

'We have more in common than you know. I lost an infant son too... but mine won't turn up in later life.'

'Jesus, I'm sorry.' Frank said, genuinely shocked. 'Does my mother know? She's certainly not told me.'

'Yes, she knows but it's not her story to tell and she's a woman of discretion.'

'You mean good at keeping secrets.' Frank smiled.

'That's true. Plum's obviously not told you either?' Apricot queried.

Frank shook his head. He'd been trying to delay bringing up the subject of Mirabelle but it was inevitable they'd talk about her at some stage.

'Plum and I met on the maternity ward in 1982 and we've been friends on and off ever since. She had Andy and I had my Clive... Clive had a hole in the heart and despite surgery he died at nine months.'

'That's awful,' Frank said.

'It was a long time ago and at the time it put a huge strain on my marriage. We divorced not long after. I never dared have another child and I never remarried, so I could never be hurt like that again. Plum understood.'

Frank didn't know how to follow that so looked to food as an escape.

'Would you like a dessert, or a brandy?' he asked.

'I'll just have a single espresso thanks.'

Over coffee, served with little squares of chocolate truffle, he dared to ask about Mirabelle and Andy.

'She's putting on a brave face but I know she misses you, Frank,' Apricot said.

'Is she dealing with Andy any better?' he asked. 'I worry about his moods and alcohol intake, having been there myself, but he wouldn't take advice from me.'

'His new boyfriend had been quite good and got him to see a doctor.'

'What, the runner? Well, that's a surprise,' Frank said.

'No, not the runner, this one's a plumber who fits kitchens and wants a joiner to help him.'

'You mean Andy is actually working? Amazing.'

'Just casual jobs at the moment but it's a start. It might develop into something regular if he doesn't mess up.'

'Fingers crossed then.'

'Oh, and the other thing, they've got back in touch with Andy's father in North Wales, somewhere near Bangor. Andy's going up to visit him next week.'

Frank felt a tightness in his throat, not exactly a lump but a strange sensation that made him want to get up and move about.

'Excuse me, I'm just popping to the gents. Do you want another coffee?'

'No, thanks. I'll not sleep and I want to be alert for tomorrow's events.'

When Frank returned, he requested the bill.

'Sorry, did I say too much?' Apricot said.

'No, it's just sad that they seem to be managing better without me,' Frank said.

'Why don't you phone her?' Apricot said.

'Why doesn't she phone me? She's the one who said goodbye.'

'What do you want, Frank? You have to make up your mind.'

'I don't know and that's the problem. I want things to be as they were. Is that too much to ask?'

'Keep an open mind and listen to your heart. It's hard work being lonely, believe me.'

Frank shrugged and heard his voice in the background.

This woman talks sense, don't be afraid to listen.

'Can I walk you back to your B and B?'

Frank asked.

'Thanks, if it's not out of your way. It's been a lovely evening. You can tell me about Maureen's garden on the way home. I hear you've done a good job.'

CHAPTER 39

Frank was looking forward to choir re-starting after the four-week break. He was mildly concerned about seeing Sharon again but there'd be enough other people around to dilute any tension. It might actually be fun to catch up with Olga and see how her summer with Mr Smit was going. Geoff would no doubt be there too and they could talk cars during the interval.

Frank walked to the rehearsal hall, which was too close to justify driving and using petrol. He needed to feel the breeze on his face after being stuck in a dusty warehouse all day. The world felt good and he hummed as he walked. He'd just had the good news in a phone call from Gus, that Sandra was in the early stages of pregnancy following their second IVF attempt. They weren't going to announce it to anyone else until after the 12 weeks scan but thought Frank should know so he didn't have to query the new items on the hospital bills. They hadn't even told Della yet, which was obviously a strain on Sandra because she'd been staying with them since her last hospital discharge. At least Della was on the mend, getting stronger and soon going back to her own bungalow.

Frank was relieved his donation to the baby-making fund had been worth it and he was pleased Della was getting better without him having forked out for her too. Hopefully they were all going to do well and the payments to the fertility service could end soon. This was good because resolving the mess of Reg's care home fees had been a more expensive exercise than he'd imagined.

Frank was beginning to wonder if early retirement might still be financially viable. Moving to Ipswich was off the agenda now and Frank had given up the idea of buying his own house in the Felixstowe area a while ago. He'd only been dreaming and really couldn't afford to buy a place, so now he was toying with the idea of renting. He'd choose somewhere nice where he could feel proud, somewhere he might like to bring a woman home to. He was going to be too early arriving at rehearsals, so walking past one of the big estate agents, he stopped to look in the window for properties to rent. The monthly prices weren't too scary - okay, more than he paid for his grotty lodgings at Docklands Road - but a couple of these two-bed flats looked appealing. He didn't yearn for ownership, just wanted a bit of an upgrade and a decent landlord or landlady. He took a picture of the ones he fancied on his phone so he could later look them up online, then carried on humming his way to choir.

There were one or two voices missing and a few newcomers had joined.

'Our leader has obviously been out canvassing,' Frank whispered to Geoff.

'I think it was the write up in the paper about the concert tour. Did you not see it?' Geoff replied.

'No, which paper?'

'Gentlemen, when you're ready please,' called the conductor, tapping his music stand sharply.

'Tell you later,' hissed Geoff.

At half-time, Frank looked around for Sharon in case she'd simply been running late but there was no sign. He didn't mind too much, nor was he bothered that Olga was busy giving the new tenor a warm welcome. *He looks more her type, more distinguished than me,* Frank thought with amusement. *Probably lives in a big house, good for him.*

'Tea or coffee, Frank? How's the car running?' Geoff patted Frank on the back.

'Tea thanks. The car's great, best thing I've ever bought. Now tell me about this article?'

'In the East Anglia Daily Times. I got it online. I've saved it so I'll try to forward you a link.'

'Thanks. I see Sharon's not here tonight. Is she okay?'

'More than okay, she's on her honeymoon.'

'What!' Frank spluttered. 'She's married?'

'Whirlwind affair, I gather, someone she met at the Book Festival swept her off her feet.'

'Just practising on me, then. Narrow escape,' muttered Frank.

'What's that?' Geoff asked.

'Nothing, just saying not such a sparrow after all.'

'Ha, you don't know the half of it, she's been on the lookout for ages,' Geoff chortled. 'Anyway, she'll be back next week.'

'Ladies and gentlemen, shall we resume?'

called the choirmaster, tapping his music stand.

Frank walked home with a sense of contentment. He'd enjoyed stretching his lungs and exercising his vocal cords and now couldn't wait for next week's session when he might hear more about Sharon. Back in his room, he checked his emails and found the article from Geoff. It was full of praise and enthusiasm for community choirs, quoting how good they were for mental health and all age groups. It particularly stressed that new choir members would be welcome and there was a picture of the group attached. Frank had forgotten it being taken. He stood taller than most of the other men and thought he looked quite handsome. He planned to ask at work if he could use the printer in one of the offices to get a copy for his mother. Frank was aiming to drive up to see her at the weekend. She was recovering well after her knee replacement, so they'd soon be discussing plans for her discharge.

He looked at the estate agent's website and found the details of the two apartments he'd earmarked.

The following morning, he rang to book a viewing for the one he preferred.

'We've had had a number of enquiries already, Sir. We're arranging viewings this Saturday, there's a slot available at 3 pm.'

'Are any other days? I'm busy on Saturday.'

'Nothing until the following weekend, Sir. I suspect it'll be gone by then.'

'Bugger! I mean sorry, that's difficult but I'll take the 3 pm appointment thank you.'

'Name and contact details?

'Frank Roberts.' He gave his mobile phone number.

'I'll meet you there, Mr Roberts. My name is Jude.'

He put the phone down and immediately called Maureen to rearrange for his visit for Sunday.

'They're sending me home Monday,' she announced. You might as well leave it until I'm home. Cathy's going to stay with me for the first week and then we'll see how things go.'

'I'm really busy next week, Mum, I've got shifts at work, a dental appointment and then there's choir. I'm not sure I can rearrange them all. No, I'll still come Sunday if that's all right. There's something I want to talk over with you. I'm glad you've got Cathy coming in.'

'See you on Sunday then. Must go - lunch is here.'

She sounds all right. No need to feel guilty, she's managed without you for long enough.

CHAPTER 40

Frank took a drive to look at the outside of the apartment. On the neat residential road, he saw the building; two small balconies upstairs on the front and there were entrance doors down a path to the left-hand side. Frank deduced there were probably two flats on the ground floor and two on the first floor. He wondered if the balcony was big enough to sit and have a cup of tea on, or was it just for pot plants? The narrow communal garden at the front seemed well cared for and the external paintwork in good condition. He'd been led to believe the building was owned by a property developer and the apartments were rented out on annually renewable leases, managed by the estate agent. All good, he thought, at least I won't have to deal with the likes of Mrs West.

On the day of his viewing, Frank arrived early and parked a little way up the road. He sat and watched a young couple being escorted out by an even younger person, wearing in a stylish grey suit. *That must be Jude*, he thought, she looks as if she could be Miss Freeman's younger sister. As the couple walked away, Frank realised the woman was heavily pregnant as she leaned on her partner's arm. *Oh goodness, they probably need this place more than I do*, he thought, but then considered it might be too small for them and difficult living on the first floor having to carry car seats and prams and all that baby stuff up and down. *I'm still in with a chance*, he decided, as he strode to meet the agent.

'Mr Roberts, I presume, pleased to meet you,' she said. 'We can go straight in. I presume you've had time to go through the details but ask me anything you want.'

'Thanks,' said Frank, following Jude up the stairs. 'Steeper than I expected.' He wondered if he'd ever get his mother up the stairs to visit.

'That's what the last couple said. Good handrails though and wide enough.'

'And not lime green with a snake at the top,' Frank said with a wry smile.

Jude looked puzzled. Frank just kept smiling and shrugged his shoulders.

'Yes, well, it's in excellent condition, as you can see,' said Jude, 'and the landlords always have their apartments deep cleaned on changeover. New kitchen here,' she pointed out. 'The boiler's been recently replaced too.'

'Very nice,' said Frank.

'Here's the spacious living room, smaller bedroom number two is next, and the main bedroom is at the end with the little Juliet balcony.'

'Juliet?' Frank queried.

'Yes, it's just for appearances.'

'Oh, I see, too small to stand on.' Frank's face fell as he entered the room.

Jude led him out quickly. 'Nice electric shower in the bathroom next door, as you can see and that's about all I have to show you. Would you like to wander around on your own?'

'No, it's fine. I've seen all I need.'

'Will it just be you living here?'

'Yes, just me.' Frank tried to make the statement sound positive.

'I'd say perfect for a single person. Easy to run but the spare room giving flexibility, maybe for conversion to a study? You do know there's no pets allowed?'

'Not a problem.'

Frank was amused at the idea he might need a study. He didn't want a pet but the stairs still worried him, and another thing, he'd always lived in institutions or shared accommodation before and had never actually lived alone. He gave his best enthusiastic expression and told Jude he was genuinely interested and he'd be in touch soon.

'Make it very soon,' she said. 'Monday at the latest, I'd say. This one'll go quickly,' said Jude with a cheery smile.

I bet they always say that.

For the rest of the day, Frank fretted over what to do. This was a huge decision. He took out the notebook, grimaced at the cat on the cover and wrote a list of questions, pros and cons.

Would renting the flat finally shut the door on moving to Ipswich and living with Mirabelle? No, he would only be committed here for twelve months, and that door was probably closed anyway.

Could he imagine staying at Docklands Road until the end of time? No, he bloody well hoped not.

Could he run a home by himself? Yes,

Mirabelle had improved his household skills no end.

Would he be lonely living on his own? No, as it was, he hardly talked to his present landlady or Carlos.

Yes, he'd enjoy pottering in the garden and might offer to look after it for the other residents to save on the maintenance fee.

Yes, he'd have proper neighbours to talk to and he might even have a balcony.

In the end, he decided he didn't need much to make it his own. He could get second-hand furniture and household stuff from the charity shops in town or maybe his mother would have some hand-me-downs.

He drove to Lowestoft early, planning to tidy up the garden for Maureen's homecoming before going in to visit.

'What the...?' he exclaimed, as he approached and saw Apricot's car parked in the road outside.

He pulled up quickly and jumped out. Apricot opened the front door with a Cheshire-cat-smile.

'What the heck are you doing here?' Frank asked.

'Getting it ready for Maureen to come home tomorrow. I've been tidying up and made sure there's food in the fridge. Sorry, I didn't know you were coming today. Cathy's husband didn't say.'

'What?' Frank was flummoxed.

'Her husband phoned me last night from

hospital. There's been an emergency - Cathy's broken her leg falling off a ladder. She gave him my number before she went in for surgery - she didn't have yours and he thought they'd better not panic Maureen.'

'Why did she have yours and not mine?'

'We'd met once or twice and exchanged numbers when I was visiting, thought it would come in useful, as indeed it has,' she said.

'Why didn't you phone me?' Frank said crossly. 'Does my mother know all this?'

'No, it was too late last night, I thought I'd tell her today when I'd sorted things out. I've brought enough things to stay for a week if necessary.'

'Well, I don't really know what to say, it's very kind of you but this isn't really your problem.'

'I'll go home if you don't need me. You'll be staying now, I presume?'

'I didn't say that. Actually, I might not be able to stay, I just like to be kept informed. She is my mother.'

'And she is my friend and I have more time on my hands than you. Now do you want me to stay or not?' Apricot asked firmly.

'Let's sit down calmly and think about it. Then we can go in together and ask Maureen what she wants,' Frank said, frantically back-tracking, thinking it might actually help having Apricot to stay, initially at least.

Frank never got round to tidying the garden. Apricot, of course said she'd do it if she stayed. Frank tried to be gracious even though she made him feel useless, like a spare part. He came up with a compromise; Apricot might stay one week, presuming Maureen was up for it, then Frank would cover the week after.

Frank thought it must have been the surprise of seeing him and Apricot together that made Maureen drop her cup of tea over her lap when she saw them walk into the rehabilitation unit. An orderly who must have witnessed the spillage came running but by the time she got to the bedside, Apricot had already whisked the wet throw from Maureen's knees and grabbed a jug of water from her side cabinet as if she was preparing to throw it over the hot tea. Frank just caught her elbow in time.

'I'm fine. It's okay, no harm done,' Maureen said breathlessly.

The orderly patted her soggy skirt and tidied Maureen up.

'More tea, dear?' she said, then left them to it after Maureen declined.

Frank started to laugh. 'Sorry to startle you, Mother.'

'I was expecting you on your own Frank. Are you two together now?'

'No, no way, all will be explained but first of all, how are you?' Frank smiled.

'Doing well. I can't wait to go home. The tea here is awful and as you can see, too cold to scald.' She smiled back and listened to their tale.

'Poor Cathy, how awful for her, she'll be off

312

her feet longer than me,' she said.

The ward sister came to check all was well and said they'd been able to get Maureen's medication from the pharmacy early, so if she wanted to, Maureen could go home that afternoon.

She agreed for Apricot to stay that first week and Frank to return the following weekend. After that, the care agency might have found a temporary replacement for Cathy. Apricot helped pack Maureen's belongings and not long after, she was ready to go home.

While Apricot was settling in ad making up the beds, Frank and Maureen were left alone.

'Are you sure you're happy with this? I must say Apricot seems very keen to stay,' commented Frank.

'I'm fine. She likes to feel useful and needed. It's hard living alone for some. I'm usually happier being alone but for now I have to be practical. I hear she's quite a good cook. So that's a bonus.'

'True, she'll be better than me in the kitchen,' Frank smirked.

'I thought Mirabelle had taught you some basics. Is it really all over with her?'

'I think so. Look Mum, I need your thoughts on something more immediate. I went to look at a nice flat to rent yesterday. I'm thinking of moving out of Docklands Road and getting a place of my own. What do you think?'

'Well, some people enjoy living on their own, it does give you more freedom. Tell me all the details.'

'I think I'll be better staying in Felixstowe than moving to Ipswich,' he explained after showing her the agent's bumf.

'I think it sounds very nice. Now if you can afford it, I'd say go for it,' Maureen said.

'The trouble is, I don't think you'll be able to manage the stairs if you want to come to stay one day,' Frank said.

'The physios had me doing a flight of stairs yesterday, that was one of the criteria for getting discharged. I told them I live in a bungalow and will have nowhere to practise,' she chuckled. 'Anyway, you mustn't lose a good opportunity just because of me. Besides which, how often would I visit?'

'You never know.'

'No, you can drive up and see me anytime and I'll be happy with that.'

First thing Monday morning, Frank phoned Jude from work.

'Sorry, Mr Roberts, it's gone already. We accepted a firm offer late Saturday afternoon.'

'Oh, that's a bugger,' Frank said, then went silent, not knowing what to say next.

'I know you're disappointed but we have a one-bedroom flat nearby about to become available for rent. It's just down the same road but we haven't got it ready to go in our window yet. It needs some minor work done, a new carpet and a deep clean. That might take about a week but when it's ready, I can offer you first viewing.'

'I like the location. Yes, I would be

interested,' Frank said.

'I have some preliminary details here; it's ground floor, same sort of age as that first one you looked at. I'll have to check about parking. It's got one good-sized bedroom with fitted wardrobes. The living room's not bad either. Sounds ideal for a single person.'

'I'd like to see it but I'm busy next weekend. I have to visit my elderly mother in Lowestoft.'

'That's nice,' Jude said. 'I could pencil you in for Friday afternoon and we'll keep our fingers crossed it's ready to view by then.'

This young woman must be on commission.

'If I leave work early on Friday, I could be there by four.'

'I'll put it in my diary. I'll text you the full address, confirm the details and see you there at 4 pm this Friday. Have a good week.'

That night, Frank phoned Maureen to check all was well, then revisited his worry list and adjusted the details. The rent would be cheaper for one bedroom and he could always get a sofa bed for the living room in case of guests. Ground floor might actually be better, so long as there weren't noisy upstairs neighbours. He did hope there'd be decent parking space in the road. He'd drive by again after work during the week to check it out.

CHAPTER 41

When Frank arrived in Lowestoft the following week to relieve Apricot from her duties, the garden looked tidy and full of colour. Once inside, Frank was greeted by a spotlessly clean living room and the homely smell of warm pastry. A spectacular cut-flower arrangement stood on a small side table by the window and the main dining table was set for lunch for three. Rolled napkins had been placed in dainty silver rings.

'This is going to be a hard act to follow,' Frank said cheerfully.

'How long can you stay?' his mother asked.

'I could do with getting back Thursday. I'll explain why over lunch.'

'That'll be fine, we should have a new carer in place by then,' Apricot said.

There goes that royal we again.

'She'll come in twice a day from mid-week then drop down to once a day as soon as Maureen's happy,' she continued.

'Sounds perfect. Okay with you, Mum?'

'Grand,' Maureen said. 'Now tell me your latest development on the flat.'

'I'm going for it. I had a viewing yesterday and it's just what I need. Not quite as smart as the first one but still in pretty good nick. It has its own parking space and a small outside shed. The bedroom has good storage too, with a fitted wardrobe.'

'Rent not too high, then?' Maureen queried.

'Reasonable I'd say, and it's on the ground

floor so you can visit.'

Maureen looked delighted and Frank was so relieved, he got up and gave her a hug. They were both so unfamiliar with prolonged mother and son embraces they didn't quite know what to do with themselves when it was time to separate.

The oven timer pinged, allowing Apricot to escape the awkward scene. She returned a little later from the kitchen with a steaming hot chicken pie, bowls of vegetables and three warmed plates. Frank remembered how Mirabelle always warmed the plates and had given a forgiving smile when he said he never did. He thought perhaps in his new kitchen, he would.

Maureen had a rest after lunch while Frank and Apricot cleared up in the kitchen.

'Plum phoned last evening to see how we were doing,' Apricot said.

'That's nice, I gather you've made up,' Frank said. 'How was she?'

'She said she was fine but sounded rather flat, said you hadn't spoken for a while.'

'No, I suppose not,' Frank said. 'Is there a fresh tea towel somewhere?'

'Top drawer. Plum seems to think your break is permanent, now you've stopped phoning,' Apricot explained.

'She hasn't phoned me. I thought she didn't need me around now she has Andy.'

'You're as bad as each other. I think she misses you. Do you miss her?'

'I see you're as direct as ever! Yes, I do miss

her sometimes but actually I'm enjoying getting on with life.'

'I suppose that's all right then. She's also doing well in some ways - she's had a couple of painting commissions and she's making more effort with the B and B again.'

'What, with Andy in the house? That must be a challenge,' Frank spluttered.

'He's gone.'

'What do you mean gone? Back to Australia?'

'No, gone to Wales to live with his dad.'

'Permanently? Good heavens, that's some news. What about the boyfriend? Frank said.

'The previous chap, Mel, is off the scene. Apparently, there's someone else in Wales now, so every hope he'll stay up there.'

'Blimey, he doesn't have any trouble picking up new blokes,' Frank commented.

'Well, he's a good-looking man and he can be quite nice when he's not drinking. Might even hold down a job.' Apricot said. 'I do hope so for Plum's sake.'

Frank grunted.

'Why hasn't she told me all this?' he asked after a thoughtful pause.

'I wonder?' Apricot turned to put away the pots and pans with more clattering than was entirely necessary.

'I'm going to walk round the garden,' Frank said. 'What time are you off?'

'I'll pack my bags and go once I've said cheerio to Maureen. Are you sure you can manage?'

'I'm sure.'

CHAPTER 42

Frank had felt uncertain when Maureen suggested he buy change of address cards at a gift shop in Lowestoft. He sat at his mum's table while she watched TV and wrote a list of people to inform. It was *a simple list, not tragically short*, he told himself, *not as pathetic as it might have been a year ago but short all the same.* He'd thought he only needed to inform work and the choir master but then the list grew. *Guess it was Mirabelle who'd got me into list making.*

Frank put Maureen, and Gus and Sandra's names on the list but decided to leave Della off to begin with. He added Olga, Geoff, and then Sharon with a question mark, after all he didn't know her new surname. He made a second list of officials who needed informing, like Miss Freeman, the bank, dentist and optician and that was just about it. They might have to manage with texts or phone-calls rather than cards, as he'd only bought one pack of twelve.

Look at you with your fancy cards.

Frank suddenly realised he'd left out Apricot, so quickly added her, then he gingerly wrote Mirabelle's name, she was, after all, the queen of list making. He still hadn't phoned her but thought he might slip a handwritten letter inside her card to pave the way.

Once back in Felixstowe, whilst organising his move, he gave Mirabelle a great deal of thought. He was certain getting the flat was the right thing to do, regardless of any consideration of their relationship. After all, it was she who'd once said he must stop trying to do things for others and look after himself. They could be friends again, maybe even partners but they didn't need to live together. Actually, it might be better for them both if they didn't. Would Mirabelle agree that they needed their own lives? Who knew? But he had a feeling Apricot would support it.

The days sped by and soon the deposit was paid and appropriate papers sent to the agent, along with details of three people he'd asked for references: his boss, the choirmaster and Mrs West, his soon to be ex-landlady. Maureen had given him some crockery and kitchen utensils she no longer used and a few other bits and pieces like a small folding table and a chair that he had just been able to squeeze into his car to take back to Felixstowe. He'd already put a deposit down on some other pieces of furniture in the British Heart Foundation charity shop but decided he wouldn't accept a second-hand bed. A new beginning meant a new bed and that would be delivered as soon as he got the keys. The thought of getting his own keys made him both excited and nervous. At least this was a positive move for him, unlike poor Reg when he left Chestnut Cottage to move into the care home. Hopefully Reg had been too unwell to realise what was happening.

Before Frank's departure, Mrs West checked

his room's inventory and looked crestfallen at having to return the full deposit. *Good, that'll pay for a new duvet and bedding*, Frank thought. Carlos didn't even bother to say goodbye.

He needed to make two trips in his jam-packed Fiesta to move all his stuff. Frank sang along with the car radio, his new place to sing. He'd not ever sung in the shower at Docklands Road. Things were going to change.

He hummed, 'Get ready, here I come' as he unloaded and unpacked. When evening came, he phoned the nearest Chinese restaurant for a take-way meal, the first on his own plates in his own home. Once his stomach was full of sweet and sour pork and egg fried rice, he phoned Maureen to tell her he was installed.

'Where will you sleep with no bed?' she asked, sounding just like a mother who'd worried over her son for years.

'Geoff's lent me a blow-up mattress for now and I've got a single duvet to be going on with.'

'Good. What about curtains? Have you got curtains?'

'There are blinds, I don't need curtains,' he said.

'Send me some pictures.'

'You might have to wait until I'm more organised. I'll take some as soon as it looks decent.'

'I got your change of address card this morning, very nice.'

'How's the new carer doing?' Frank asked.

'She's no Cathy but she's better than

nothing. I think you and Apricot overdid it - I hardly need her. I'm walking better each day, although it is nice to have someone around when I shower.'

'Just hang on to her until Cathy's back. I'll worry less if I know someone's calling in.'

'Hark at you,' she laughed down the phone. 'Oh, yes, Gus phoned yesterday. It sounds as if I'm doing better than poor Della. She's back in her own bungalow but Celine has to go in most days during the week.'

'That's not so good. Have you heard how Sandra is? I don't even know when she's due?' Frank asked.

'Gus was being vague about it but can't be long. She's keeping well now after a rocky start. I think that's why Celine is making herself so available to Della, to keep the pressure off Sandra.'

'I still haven't met Celine, is she nice?'

'I've only seen her once or twice but apparently she's a treasure. Della always says how marvellous she is with the Trelawney twins and is very much steadier than that sister you met.

'Yes, Tricia's a fine-looking woman but quite a character. Gus still hasn't given me the whole picture. I'd be interested to know more one day.'

'I always wondered why Gus was so pleased she moved away,' Maureen commented.

'Sandra too. Anyway, I'd better go and blow up my bed. I'll call you again soon. Goodnight.'

Frank slept poorly. The blow-up bed smelt of

rubber and squeaked whenever he moved. He felt sweaty and the Chinese meal gave him a raging thirst. He had to get up for water in the night and then was up early, watching the breakfast news on his portable TV when the postman came with a card from Maureen and a flyer from Crisis at Christmas.

He opened the Crisis leaflet first, even though Christmas was weeks away. He would not be alone this Christmas or even having to share it with Carlos, so Frank donated a Christmas meal for a person more needy. When he opened Maureen's card, his breath caught as a twenty-pound note fell out with the message 'Didn't know what to buy as a housewarming present so get something you need for your new home xx'.

Frank clutched the money to his chest.

Get a grip Frank.

Frank was pleased get rid of the smell and return the blow-up mattress to Geoff at the next choir meeting. Rehearsal started promptly, then at the interval, the ladies crowded around, fussing Frank about his new home. Geoff and the other men grinned from afar while Frank had offers of household hand-me-downs. Olga gave him a potted plant with the strict instructions not to over water it.

Sharon hovered in the background at first then gave him an envelope. 'My husband and I are moving away soon. This is our new address.'

Her red dye in her hair had faded and she

looked like a little brown sparrow again but with a bigger smile. She pecked his cheek and said, 'This is my last time at choir practice. Can I ring you at the weekend? We have some things we won't need in our new home that might be useful for you.'

'That's very kind, Sharon.'

If things had been different!

Choir finished early for once and Frank enjoyed going home to a clean and comfy flat, the furnishings and décor were coming together well. He put the pot plant on the windowsill and looked forward to a good night's sleep in his new double bed. He snapped some photos for his mother with his phone before closing the blinds. Everything looked homely in the fading light of autumn with the wall lights casting shadows. While the phone was in his hand, he tried to phone Mirabelle but it went to voicemail. He didn't leave a message.

CHAPTER 43

A few days later, another card arrived, this time from Mirabelle. It was a print of one of her paintings and inside she'd hand drawn a cartoon of a green snake with a wicked grin, climbing up a staircase and she'd written 'Good luck Frank. Thought you might enjoy this picture. Onwards and ever upwards. Miss you. Love Mirabelle x'

He propped it up on the windowsill next to Olga's pot plant, then that evening, moved it to his bedside cabinet. He picked up the phone to call Ipswich again and this time Mirabelle answered.

'Just phoning to thank you for the nice card, how are you?'

'I'm okay, you?'

The stilted initial exchange of questions and answers soon got easier. Frank was genuinely pleased to hear that Andy was doing well in Wales, getting to know his father and phoning his mother more regularly. In his absence, business was picking up, with mostly mid-week working folk staying at Mirabelle's B and B.

'Has Andy stopped drinking?' Frank asked bluntly.

'Not stopped completely but it seems more under control.'

'That's good. Are you painting?'

'Yes, I must tell you something about that. A woman called Selena Burt, or something like that, she spoke rather softly, has made contact and she wants to buy a picture she saw at the exhibition.'

'Why didn't she just buy it there?' Frank asked.

'The one she liked had a red dot so she's asked me to paint a similar scene. It's the one of the heather-covered slopes behind the lake at Bala.'

'Nice,' said Frank only vaguely remembering it; to him, they all looked the same.

'She's coming over at the weekend to confirm the commission while she's in town but I've already made a start. It's one of my favourite views anyway and I thought I'd better get on with it. She needs it by next month.'

'Tight deadline then?'

'Yes, it's a fortieth birthday present for her sister who's coming to stay.'

'Well, good luck with that. Let me know how you get on. Before you go, can you email me your pancake recipe? I thought I might try and make some, now I have my own kitchen.'

'Take care of the light fittings when you flip,' she laughed at the end of the longest conversation they'd had in weeks.

The pancake recipe arrived in Frank's email inbox late Saturday morning when he'd just finished watching Saturday Kitchen and was wondering what to eat for lunch. He was disappointed there wasn't much of a message to accompany the instructions. *So, pancakes for lunch today,* he decided, *then maybe a walk into town.* He had a weekend to himself, because Apricot was visiting Maureen.

Frank did his food shop for the coming week and added few bits of houseware to the trolley. His non-stick frying pan had lost its Teflon finish and needed replacing and his two tea towels were looking tired. He picked up a pottery salt and pepper set and last of all, added a local newspaper, primarily for the television listings.

When he got home, the sports pages at the back of the paper caught his eye. Geoff had mentioned going to watch Felixstowe and Walton F.C. so he checked out their fixtures for the new season. It jumped out at him that he now had contacts in Stowmarket, Ipswich Wanderers, and Lowestoft Town. Having lived in Felixstowe so long, why had he not taken more notice of the local teams? He used to like playing football as a youngster and pretended to support Chelsea but only to try and keep up with other lads at school.

When he first worked at the docks, some people had mistaken him for a professional footballer because apparently, he looked rather like one of the Ipswich Town players, but he hadn't bothered to support the team or any other in the area. He never thought he'd stay long in Felixstowe but here he was, nearly twenty years later, setting down real roots. Perhaps he should now consider the local footballing scene. It would be a good start to get the paper more regularly and keep an eye on the fixtures. It would give him something else to talk about at work, where to be honest, he didn't have many friends and those he had weren't much interested in the choir. He wondered if Maureen knew anything about Lowestoft Town. After all, she'd lived there all her life. He imagined his mysteriously absent father might even have gone to the footie. Now he and Maureen were closer, he could carefully quiz her for more information about his missing father.

After the weekend, Mirabelle phoned.

'Good news - I've got that commission sorted. The woman seemed a really nice,' Mirabelle gabbled excitedly.

'That's good,' Frank said.

'Brilliant, you mean?' she teased.

'Tell me more,' Frank said.

'She was very polite and didn't quibble at the price, even though I'd put it up a notch.'

'How much?'

'I'm not telling. She told me her sister went to North Wales on holiday last year with her partner and they drove through Bala. She's raved about the colours of the heather and the mountains beyond the lake ever since. Anyway, what's-her-name Burt seems to think her sister might be announcing her engagement on her actual birthday, so she wanted something really special to give her and she remembered my painting.'

'Well, that is exciting for you. Congratulations,' Frank said.

'And she gave me a cash deposit. I'm to let her know when it's ready to collect. She doesn't live in town, so we might have to arrange a delivery.'

'You clever old thing,' Frank chuckled.

'Less of the old, thank you,' Mirabelle replied.

Frank opened his mouth before he thought through what came next. He'd missed this happy, excitable version of Mirabelle and wanted to hear more of it.

'Actually, Mirabelle, I wondered if you'd like to come over and see the flat, once it's a bit more organised?'

'I'd love to, when were you thinking? It'll have to be a weekend, because my house guests usually come midweek.'

'I've promised to go to Mum's next weekend, so maybe the following Saturday. Shall I come and collect you?' Frank asked.

'No. I'll get the bus. I can be with you in time for lunch.'

Frank loved the way her days revolved around food. He realised he'd have to prepare something enticing to eat. He wondered whether to try and expand his repertoire of recipes, or maybe he should just get a takeaway. He wondered how long she'd stay. *Would it be wise to change the sheets just in case?*

'Are you still there, Frank?' she queried.

'Yes, sorry, just thinking. Ask the driver for the pier bus stop. Let me know what time and I'll meet you there.'

When he put the phone down, his heart was jumping about like a grasshopper. Had he made a mistake? Why complicate life again? Things were going along smoothly, falling into place. He had money, friends, new neighbours, a car and most significantly, he had his mother. Oh goodness, what would his mother think? He wouldn't mention Mirabelle's impending visit, she would ask too many questions but if he didn't tell her and Mirabelle told Apricot, the news might get to her anyway.

You only asked her to come and see the flat, you haven't asked her to marry you. And you'd better make the place shipshape.

CHAPTER 44

Frank managed to avoid discussing his relationship with Mirabelle on his next weekend visit to see his mother. He was kept busy, helping with her shopping, clearing some autumn growth in the garden and sweeping leaves from the front path. When they sat down to eat in the evening, Frank started talking football.

Some of Maureen's Brownies had been keen on the game and had formed a girls' team in the 80s. They couldn't find many other teams to play, so it didn't last but by then some of them were playing at school. Maureen liked supporting her girls but wasn't really a football fan. She had little or no idea what Lowestoft Town were up to.

While she was telling Frank about the footballing girls, she volunteered it wasn't Reg's thing either. Frank pursued the subject.

'I played a bit a school,' he said, 'mainly in defence. What about my father? Was he a player?'

'Not that I knew. If he was, it would have been American Football - a very different game. We didn't talk about things like that.'

'American!' Frank gasped. How stupid, of course, Reg had told him it was an American boyfriend who'd broken her heart. "Why won't you tell me anything about him?'

'Because I'm ashamed... ashamed to say I didn't know him very well and I haven't much to tell you.'

'Oh, heavens, did he, you know, take advantage of you?'

'It wasn't really like that. I knew the time would come when I might have to tell you. I think these days they'd call it a casual, one-night stand. He was handsome, tall, dark haired with blue eyes like yours. I was young and stupid and as much to blame as him.'

'And...?'

'Here goes. He was based at RAF Lakenheath. We met at a village dance in Bungay. They'd bussed in lots of bored Americans from the base. I remember the Americans called it a jam; we Brits called it a hop. Jimmy was one of the younger GIs and a great dancer. The girlfriend I'd gone with went off with one of his friends, so it seemed acceptable to do the same. It was fun. I thought we'd just have a kiss and a cuddle but it ended as rather more than that. On the way home, my friend and I both agreed not to tell a soul how foolish we'd been. Trouble is, I was caught out and she wasn't.'

'Did you see him again? Did he know about me?'

'He never called me. I tried to contact him at the RAF base when I discovered I'd fallen pregnant and they couldn't tell me who or where he was. They needed a surname and I only knew his first name was Jimmy and he had dark brown hair and smiling eyes. He talked with a slight stammer.'

'Jimmy,' said Frank. 'Jimmy with a stammer and smiling blue eyes. Is that all? Did you eventually manage to trace him?'

'No, my friend said her fella had gone back to America at the end of his posting in England and it was assumed Jimmy was in the same batch. She said she'd try to find out about Jimmy for me but I never heard from her again.'

'So that was that. It's really sad. He's out there somewhere, probably in the US, a man who knows nothing about your situation or my existence. Oh well, thanks for telling me, it can't have been easy.'

'I'm fine. I've got on with life and now I've found you, which is all that matters. You can perhaps see why I was reticent and didn't want this aired in public. Imagine having to face the judgement of someone like Della,' Maureen seemed forced to Frank.

'I can see why but I really want to ask you some more questions, if you don't mind.'

'Maybe tomorrow, I've had enough for tonight.' Maureen yawned her way to bed.

Frank stayed up and jotted notes in his journal and tried to process the facts. Poor Maureen, he kept thinking. Jimmy, I wonder? He guessed it was her shame that made her give up the search so easily and shun his own attempts to make contact with her. She had no need to feel ashamed.

Maureen washed up the breakfast things; Frank dried and put them away while they talked.

'Is there anything else you can tell me? How

old do you think Jimmy was when you met and which part of the US did he come from?'

'For some reason I always thought he was from Texas but then I didn't know the name of many other states back then. Texas just stuck in my mind.'

'Anything else about the dance?'

'There were lots of US airmen, mostly young chaps from Lakenheath and a few from Mildenhall. I'm sure Jimmy was stationed at Lakenheath.'

'You did do some talking then,' Frank commented.

'Mostly it was dancing.'

'And smooching?'

Maureen blushed and fussed with the dishes. 'Do you wonder I've kept it to myself all this time?'

'Sorry. Tell me about the music?'

'Oh, we danced to Bill Haley, Frank Sinatra and that woman... what was she called? I know, Rosemary Clooney and of course Elvis Presley. It was mostly artists to please the Americans. Rosemary Clooney had a big hit back then and I seem to recall him commenting his mother's name was Rosemary.'

'This is progress. Now we know he was a brown-haired, handsome, blue-eyed American with a stammer and a mother called Rosemary, who might come from Texas. See if anything else comes to mind while I take the garden rubbish to the tip. Won't be long,'

During the next week at work, Frank couldn't stop thinking about his American father. It must have set Maureen thinking too, because the next time he went up she'd told him she'd dug out some old letters she'd kept from her teenage years.

'I was wondering if my old friend Sheila was still around. She persuaded me to go to the dance with her. We were best friends but then her mother didn't want us to see each other after that. Anyway, their family moved to Luton.'

'Luton? Why Luton? Frank said.

'Something to do with her dad's work.'

'And that's why you never heard from Sheila again? What was her surname?'

'Grimshaw, Sheila Grimshaw. I expect she got married and changed her name. Could be dead by now.'

'Cheerful thought,' he said, adding Sheila's name to his notebook.

'You look more like a policeman than a dockworker,' Maureen frowned, then rapidly changed the subject. 'Do you have pictures hanging in your flat yet?'

'No, the walls are quite bare.'

'I wonder if you'd like this?' she said bringing out a small, framed watercolour from the side of her armchair.

'You've painted this?' Frank queried. 'I love it, thank you.'

'It's of one of the places I used to go walking - Lowestoft Harbour.'

'How did you end up back in Lowestoft?

According to Reg, you didn't grow up or go to school here. I've been so busy quizzing you about my father, I've not asked enough about you and your childhood. Was it a happy one?'

'My mother was strict, especially after we lost Father, but we were never beaten or abused if that's what you're asking. We always had food on the table and a roof over our heads.'

Frank made himself comfortable in the other armchair. He could feel a long story coming on.

'I was sad when Mother got the housekeeper job at Trelawney Manor. Before that she cleaned for the Grimshaws.' Maureen paused to put her thoughts in order. 'I had to change schools when we moved to the countryside, I was only in the infants but I missed my friends. Sheila and I wrote little letters to each other and then, when I was old enough, I'd go back and stay with the Grimshaws from time to time. They were well off and used to be very kind. I think they felt sorry for me, stuck away in a country house, miles away from anywhere. They treated me like a second daughter.'

'How extraordinary that you should all lose contact.'

'You could say that. I was staying with them the weekend of the dance. They dropped me like a stone when they found out I was in the family way.'

'That's awful and you lost touch with Sheila too?'

'I'm afraid so.'

'But you managed to get back and spend

your adult life in Lowestoft?'

'Not for a while though. Mother sent me away to a home for fallen girls in Colchester to have you.'

'Was it actually called that?' Frank sighed thinking of some of the girls he'd met in children's homes in the past.

'No, they called it something slightly more obtuse but that's what it was. Reg and everyone else were kept in the dark, then when I'd got over the birth Mum had saved enough for me to go to college. I think she wanted me out of her sight. At least I'd done well at school and I got a place to train as a librarian. That led to a job at Lowestoft Library and the rest, as they say, is history.'

'My goodness, this is a lot to take in. Did you get back in touch with Sheila's parents?'

'No, they lived in Luton by then.'

'You've not had it easy, have you?' Frank took his mother's hand.

'Neither have you, Frank but you've done okay and I feel quite at home here in Lowestoft.'

'Thanks, that's good. Let's take a break. Any more jobs for me while I'm here? I have to get off in good time in the morning, I'm on a late shift starting at two.'

'Your shifts are confusing,' Maureen said. 'I'll never get my head around them.'

'I know, but I'll plod on. I thought I'd retire early but now I have the flat to finance I might wait a little longer and see how the money goes. I'll be getting the final payment from

Reg's estate soon, so long as Sandra's pregnancy stays the course.'

'I do hope all's well there. They've been rather quiet lately.'

'At least Della's improving.'

'I'll phone her tomorrow when you've gone. Do you think I ought to try and visit her before winter?'

'It's a thought. I could drive you down and you could check out my place on the same trip - maybe stay overnight.'

'I thought you only had one bedroom. Della could put me up in her spare room.'

'I told you, I've invested in a sofa bed for the living room for this very reason. You can have my bed and I'll sleep in the living room. That'd be fine for a short stay.'

'Well, you might have to toss a coin. I've never had people vying to have me to stay before,' Maureen laughed.

'Steady on... Della hasn't offered yet.'

CHAPTER 45

Frank joined Facebook. He'd always been cautious about his privacy and steered clear of social media platforms in the past but now realised it could come in handy for tracing people, maybe even old ladies like Sheila Grimshaw. He thought he'd better practise how to use it rather than dive in as a complete novice, so he searched for Mirabelle Jones. He was amazed to see how many women had that name. He was tempted to look up Tricia but wasn't sure he'd heard her surname when the police took her away. He tried Gus Hall instead and found there were even more with that name than Mirabelle Jones. Maybe this wasn't such a brilliant idea after all. He decided to leave it and ask Mirabelle's advice when she came at the weekend.

It was a bright day, so he decided to walk to the pier to meet her bus that Saturday morning. He caught a glimpse of bright purple hair though the window as the bus drew up. He went to help her down the step to the pavement then stood back in amazement.

'Wow! You look great!'

'Thank you kindly. I treated myself to a new coat with the profits from my art.' She smiled and did a Mirabelle twirl before handing him a large carrier bag.

'House-warming gift - open it later,' she added, throwing the strap of her oversized handbag across her shoulder. 'Are we walking?'

'Yes, the flat's not far. Thanks for this. You've done something else, haven't you,' he asked.

'Had a hairdo, you mean?'

'You know what I mean, I don't want to say the wrong thing but you look ten years younger.'

'You mean I looked like an old bag last time you saw me in the flesh?'

'Stop teasing. You know what I'm thinking.'

'You're thinking the fat bird has lost some weight, aren't you?'

'I wouldn't have put it quite like that, but yes and it really suits you. Oh God, you're not ill, are you?'

'No, dear Frank, I am fine. I did drop a few pounds with stress when Andy was around, and losing you didn't help, if I'm honest...' Mirabelle paused.

'You haven't really lost me, Mirabelle,' Frank said, horrified that she was so affected.

'But now I'm fine, I've perked up again and I'm just eating more healthily. Andy's settled himself and I realise I still have you as a friend. It was clear I needed to lose weight after injuring my leg.'

'Seriously, it's great to see you again,' Frank said.

'You too, Frank.'

'I thought we'd go to the flat first then maybe I'll show you the sights of Felixstowe after lunch.'

'Sounds good. One of the advantages of

losing a few kilogrammes is that I can walk further without getting so many aches and pains.'

'Don't get too skinny, though.'

'I won't. I need to keep the wrinkles pumped up and I do still like my cakes and desserts. By the way, there's a cake for you in that bag, as well as a present. I haven't asked properly how you are. I only get vague updates from Apricot but I gather Maureen's doing well.'

'I'm well and so is Mum. I have so much to tell you but here we are, this is my new abode.'

He opened up and led Mirabelle into the cosy flat, where he'd purposely left the heating on low. Frank could smell the casserole he'd prepared, cooking in the second-hand slow cooker Sharon gave him, having received a new one as a wedding present.

'This is really nice, Frank. Do I need to take my boots off indoors?'

'No need,' he said, taking her coat. 'I'll put the kettle on.'

'Do I get a guided tour?'

'It'll take about three minutes to show you round, I'll open my present first.'

'I think you already know what it is.'

'The size and shape are a bit of a giveaway. I'll explore the cake first.'

The cake was foil-wrapped and heavily scented with citrus; lemon drizzle was one of his favourites. Next, he started to unwrap the main present, a large square picture.

'It's not Ricky the cat, is it?' he chuckled.

'As if. I hope you like it.'

CHAPTER 46

'Thanks for a nice day on Saturday. I have information,' Mirabelle gabbled excitedly when she called a few days later.

'My pleasure and thanks for the picture. I've hung it where you suggested. It looks great. Now, what have you discovered?'

'There's a business called Grimshaw and Co. in Stevenage - that's not too far from Luton. The internet says Stevenage is, and I quote, "a New Town in Hertfordshire with a significant industrial area and a large number of medium-sized businesses and enterprises". So I looked at Grimshaw and Co. and found the CEO is called George Grimshaw.' Mirabelle sounded triumphant.

'No, surely it can't be that easy?'

'Maybe not. George Grimshaw doesn't fit any of the profiles on Facebook so I couldn't message him directly and I can't find him anywhere else.'

Frank groaned.

'Hang on, I've not finished. The website had an ad, they're hiring clerical staff so I called their number saying I wanted to know more about the company before I applied.'

'You are a devious woman,' Frank laughed. 'What did you discover?'

'George is only CEO in name. His son Ethan George Grimshaw runs the show now and would you believe it, he's a town councillor so I looked him up and his details are in the public domain.'

'I'm feeling a bit uncomfortable about this spying,' Frank said.

'It's not spying, it's public information. I'm not telling lies - I might well be looking for a job.'

'Are you?' Frank said in amazement.

'Not really, but I could be. Anyway, now we know who he is, you can write legitimately to Ethan George and say your mother is an old friend of Sheila, his father's cousin and she is keen to re-establish contact with her.'

'I suppose that would be all right,' Frank said. 'He's not going to just give me her address though.'

'Probably not but he might give you Sheila's married name or say he'll ask her to contact you. It's worth a try,' Mirabelle said. 'I'm afraid I couldn't access the Lakenheath archive though. I think you have to be a family member and be able to give certain details I didn't have. I didn't want to lie to the RAF.'

Frank snorted at the idea. 'No, we could do without a court case.'

'Maybe we could explore the RAF site together next time we meet,' she said.

'We're meeting again, are we?' Frank chuckled.

'I thought we might. Next time you have a day off, you could drive over here for lunch and we can carry on our research.'

'That'd be nice. You're good at this, I think you've missed your true calling in life. I meant to say, don't report back to Apricot yet, I'm not going to tell Mum until we know more and you know Apricot often phones her.'

'Got it. Won't say a word.'

Frank got a standard reply from Ethan's office to say Councillor Grimshaw would give his request his attention in due course. Probably checking out the story with Sheila, that is if she's still around, Frank thought. He fiddled around on Facebook and searched more bravely for names he knew. He rather wished he hadn't when he came across Olga Smit's page and found a picture of her in a very revealing low-cut dress, showing more of her breasts than was suitable for a woman of her age and size. Sharon's page was overflowing with sunsets and pictures of her hanging onto the arm of a much younger man. Apricot's page was, needless to say, discreet.

He couldn't resist a closer look at Mirabelle's, once he found the right Mirabelle Jones, and scrolled down over the months and years she been on the site. There were numerous pictures of her art and many of Ricky the cat, then some older ones of Andy as a youngster. He was positively pretty as a teenager, quite slightly built back then. Been on the bodybuilding supplements since, Frank guessed. He knew a bloke at work who'd got into a real mental health disaster after taking illegal supplements. He wondered whether he should alert Mirabelle or just keep the idea to himself now things were improving between them.

He was beginning to think this social media

stuff wasn't so bad and bravely took a look at Ethan George Grimshaw's page. Hidden amongst the civic stuff there was a huge group photo of a Grimshaw wedding. It appeared to be Ethan's marriage and was taken some years ago. Various names were conveniently tagged beneath the picture and Frank couldn't believe his eyes when he saw the name Sheila Bramwich, with née Grimshaw in brackets.

Frank realised he might not have to wait for Ethan's reply to his letter. He looked up Sheila Bramwich and found she was a teacher from Luton, who in her retirement, had become a well-known storyteller. She had her own website, wrote books for children and sometimes took her stories into schools and libraries across the South of England.

'Well, Mrs Sheila Bramwich, I wonder what stories you have to tell about my father and his American friends,' Frank muttered to his screen. 'You might you even have brought some of your stories to Suffolk.'

Talking to yourself isn't good for you, Frank.

Frank could hardly contain himself. He couldn't decide whether to phone Maureen or Mirabelle. He settled on Mirabelle.

'This is amazing, Frank, well done you. You don't need me at all.'

'I don't know about that. You got me started but I'm not sure where to go from here. Is it time to bring Apricot in on this? Her librarian contacts could be helpful and we'll ask her not to tell Maureen yet. I want to introduce the subject of searching for Jimmy to Mum in my

350

own time,' Frank explained.

'Actually, I think Apricot would be a great help. I'll invite her for lunch when you next come and we can tell her to zip her lips with Maureen.'

'There's a thought.' Frank loved the way Mirabelle made him laugh.

One lunchtime the following week, Mirabelle and Apricot were full of excitement about a planned outing to deliver the newly completed painting. Mirabelle proudly showed him the work she'd done for Selena Burt.

'We're about to wrap it up. Apricot offered to drive me to drop it off tomorrow and then I can get paid,' Mirabelle said.

'I could do it with you this afternoon if you want?' Frank offered.

'No, it's fine. We've arranged it all now and we're expected tomorrow. It'll be a nice drive,' Mirabelle said.

Apricot almost purred, smiling as if she'd won first prize at a cat show.

'You girls ganging up on me again?' he said in an attempt to make light of the mild rejection. He remembered the hot-and-cold Mirabelle who'd walked with him in Christchurch Park before their split and realised maintaining their friendship was more important than risking another rift.

Don't be mean, Frank, Apricot's got no-one else.

'Selina Burt lives on the way to Framlingham and we thought we'd take in the castle after the drop off. We've got the postcode and the name of her cottage,' Mirabelle told him.

You can't argue with that, Frank.

After lunch, they got down to business. Apricot had vaguely heard of the children's writer called Sheila Bramwich, so looked her up and suggested she might be able to make contact through her work at the library. They all agreed that an approach from Apricot explaining the situation might be better received than a direct attack from Frank. Frank was finding it hard to stay calm and patient so, more to distract Frank than actually expecting a helpful result, the three friends went onto the Lakenheath website after lunch. Frank paid a fee and they managed to put together enough ID and info to gain access to the archive.

1956 was thought to be the year Jimmy and his pal were posted there. It was the year of an awful nuclear accident when a B-47 bomber crashed on a training mission. When Frank read about the crash his face fell, had his father been killed? When he learned that many younger, uninvolved GIs were sent back to the US after the accident, it made him feel only slightly more hopeful.

'He'd have been named if he'd been killed in the crash,' Mirabelle reassured him.

'I suppose so,' Frank agreed. 'A lot happened in 1956. That was the year I was conceived. I need some fresh air,' Frank said. 'You two stay here, I won't be long.'

His father's probable existence was becoming a reality but even if he was still alive, their worlds were literally miles apart. Did he want to find out much more? What would he do with the information and what would Maureen think?

Frank left soon after Apricot, accepting he was not going to be invited to stay overnight with Mirabelle. He drove away happy that the day had been enjoyable and successful with new information but he remained unsettled. He was looking forward to a night at home with a film he'd got ear-marked on TV, then he might finish a book he wanted to return to Maureen when he next saw her.

Mirabelle phoned Frank the following afternoon. She was on speakerphone.

'Apricot's here, Frank and we've just got back from Framlingham,' she announced.

'Thanks for lunch yesterday, how was the castle?' Frank asked.

'Yes, good.' Mirabelle said sounding impatient and Frank wondered what he'd done wrong now.

'We've made our delivery,' Mirabelle said.

'We found the cottage,' Apricot shrieked in the background.

'And would you believe it, it's on the edge of the Trelawney estate,' Mirabelle said.

'Delightful cottage,' Apricot chipped in.

'Yes, lovely and the woman was just as nice as when I first met her,' Mirabelle said.

'Mind you, she kept us in the hall, didn't invite us right in. She opened the picture on a little hall table, and Plum had wrapped it so very carefully.'

'It was fine, she didn't want her dog to get out, anyway she loved the picture and I gave her my bank details for an online transfer before we went off to explore the castle.'

'Okay you two, what's the big deal? Frank asked.

'Tell him about when we got home,' Apricot said.

'I checked my bank statement on my phone and the money had been transferred but in the name of Celine Bird, not Selena Burt.'

Both women spluttered with laughter. Frank was rendered speechless as the penny dropped.

That's it, Bird... her name was Tricia Bird. How could you forget?

'I keep telling Mirabelle she's going deaf,' Apricot announced.

'Perhaps that's why I like your singing so much, Frank.' Mirabelle chuckled.

'Have you two been at the sherry?' Frank said, gathering his thoughts. 'I can't believe it, Celine Bird, of all people! That means the painting must be for her sister Tricia. That's bloody unbelievable.'

'Amazing, isn't it?' Mirabelle said more calmly.

'At least you got well paid, and you both enjoyed the castle. You two should form a double act,' Frank said before he signed off.

He couldn't relax. He thought Mirabelle might be phoning with information about his dad, not chit-chat about Celine and Tricia. Gus had never got round to filling him in with Tricia's story, perhaps now was a good time to ask him again?

Frank rang Gus on the pretext of asking after Della and then suggested that now he had a car, he could drive over on the coming Sunday afternoon. Maybe Gus would show him the gardens and the autumn colours in the arboretum at Lawn House which he remembered so fondly.

CHAPTER 47

Frank cleaned and polished his car on Sunday morning, and then ironed his purple and blue checked shirt, ready for his afternoon outing to Eastland. Now he'd got the postcode of Chestnut Cottage from Gus, Frank was confident that he'd find his way there. Gus had told him that Della was back in her own bungalow. Sandra would be spending the afternoon relaxing with Celine and Lynn so it would just be him at home. Gus said he was meant to be catching up with some office work but would take a break to quickly show Frank the gardens.

Frank parked in the driveway near Chestnut Cottage and looked across the lawns to the main house. Everything looked different after 20 years. The ivy that had once climbed up the walls of the house had gone and Frank didn't recognise the fading purple and pink shrubs providing the last spread of colour in front of the house. The main drive to the house had been re-surfaced and everything looked smart and neatly cared for, despite the fact that before long the autumn leaves would be falling.

'You must have an army of gardeners to keep this up to standard,' Frank said when Gus opened the door to the cottage.

Gus looked pleased with the comment. 'Afternoon, Frank. I'll get my fleece and then we can have a cup of tea in the café before we walk the gardens.'

'I see you're still open to the public.' Frank

said.

'We stay open all year if we can.' Gus replied.

'It's the arboretum I most want to see.'

'Everybody wants to see the trees. Tea first, then we'll go through the rose gardens. The roses are nearly over now but you'll see the beginning of the autumn display beyond.'

Over tea, Gus told Frank that Sandra was taking early maternity leave and resting a lot now, because they were having to watch the baby's growth. Celine was a great help with the housework at Chestnut Cottage, as well as keeping an eye on Della at the bungalow. Gus didn't ask Frank anything about his situation, his work or Mirabelle or even his mother, and Frank wasn't surprised about that. Gus was in charge here, on his own territory and seemed to be enjoying showing off to Frank.

As they walked through the gardens, Frank noticed Gus nod and acknowledge the other members of staff on duty. It looked if he was acting a part. Gus smiled at the other visitors walking around and told Frank this was all part of his job, overseeing the estate when the owner was away.

The arboretum was more magnificent than Frank remembered, for he'd only ever seen it in summer before. Now in early October, the leaves on the oaks and chestnut trees were beginning to turn golden brown, the acers' leaves were deeply red and yellow, standing out against the evergreen spruce and pine. The weeping beech, the alder and rowan trees were stunning in their russet and gold colours.

'This is wonderful,' Frank said, looking up to the clouds drifting above the highest trees.

'Glad you're impressed.' Gus's phone rang. 'Wander about for a minute while I take this.'

'Everything all right?' Frank asked when Gus had finished his call.

'Just Celine asking me to lend them a strimmer. The one they had is broken.' Gus started to walk back towards Chestnut Cottage.

'You and Sandra sound very close to Celine, unlike with Tricia. Once you told me you'd fill me in,' Frank said, striding to catch up.

Gus looked awkward. 'I did, didn't I? Why are you so interested?

'I recently met Jacob and his family in the park in Stowmarket and it reminded me of that to-do in the car park, then out of the blue, Mirabelle sold Celine a painting as a present to give to Tricia. Tricia just seems to keep cropping up.'

'She does that,' Gus said. 'She gets into people's heads. I suppose this is as good a place as any to tell you. This was Dad's favourite place after all. I'll make it brief.'

'Tell me how she got to be looking after Jacob?' Frank asked.

'Celine was a live-in nanny for Oliver's twins after their mum died.'

'And Celine is great, right?' Frank asked.

'A gem. She and Tricia were half-sisters, same mum, different fathers. They'd grown apart though.' Gus paused and took a deep breath. 'Tricia had been a child-minder in Manchester and she lost her job, so she contacted Celine and asked if she could come a stay a while. It was just when Jenny was going back to work, having had Jacob.'

'How do Jenny and Max fit in?' Frank asked.

'They're old friends of Oliver, and godparents to the twins, as am I.'

'Okay.'

'Celine lived at Lawn House in those days, so Tricia ended up renting a spare room to stay in and she often took Jacob there. She took a fancy to Oliver, who she spotted as a rich landowner. When he rejected her advances, she started playing tricks as pay back. The trouble was when her nasty games went wrong, she made it look as if my dad was to blame.'

'I'm beginning to understand why everyone's so wary of her,' Frank said.

'That's only the half of it. When she couldn't have Oliver, she made a play for me.'

'But you were already with Sandra, weren't you?'

'Yes. I loved Sandra then and still do, but like a fool, I fell for Tricia's advances.'

'Oh, Gus, that's bad.'

'Do you think I don't know?' Gus snapped. 'The twins were at school one particular day, and Celine had gone shopping. I remember it as if it was yesterday. Tricia and I were having a quick shag while Jacob was napping in the nursery next door. We were interrupted by the baby alarm. We rushed in to find he'd stopped breathing.'

'Jesus!'

'We did resuscitation while the ambulance came. The hospital called it a near cot death, caused by the shock of a poisonous spider bite.'

'I've never heard anything like it! Are there poisonous spiders in Suffolk?' Frank asked.

'Brought in with a bunch of bananas.'

'Bloody hell. Poor Jenny and Max. No wonder everyone wanted Tricia back in Manchester.'

'Baby Jacob had a nasty infection of his arm which took ages to recover. My relationship with Sandra took even longer. There's been a lot of healing to do around here.' Gus suddenly turned to face Frank. 'And that's why the bloody will hasn't helped, when we were all just getting back on an even keel.'

'I'm sorry,' Frank said quietly, 'but it's helpful to have a better idea of what's gone on. I'm pleased you and Sandra are good now and the baby is on the way. I'm glad I've found my Mum and a new family.'

'I've got to go soon to take the strimmer and I'll walk back with Sandra.'

They arrived at Chestnut Cottage in silence. Frank was aware that Gus was affected by telling this story, so didn't hang around. He thanked Gus for the tour and the chat and climbed into his car. He set off without even putting the radio on. In the wing mirror he saw Gus turn without so much as a wave.

CHAPTER 48

Frank was determined not to think any more about Tricia after that. He and Mirabelle phoned each other more often now to catch up on the progress of their slow but hopeful investigations about Jimmy.

Frank was finding it hard not to pour it all out to Maureen when he called her so instead, he focussed on his simmering friendship with Mirabelle. Maureen in return was able to report that she'd had a phone call from Della, who sounded brighter and soon Gus was going to bring her up for a visit to Lowestoft. Meanwhile, she said Celine was helping and she sounded like Wonder Woman.'

Frank wondered whether to tell his mum about his conversation with Gus but decided against it.

'And how's your Wonder Woman?' Frank asked instead.

'Cathy? Oh, it's lovely to have her back. I told her what you called her. Now you just take care with Mirabelle, good woman though she is, you don't want to get your fingers burned twice.'

'I'll be careful. Thanks for the advice, Mother,' he replied, thinking it was odd to receive this advice from a woman who'd never actually had a relationship, at least not one he'd heard of.

'Tell you what though, Apricot's gone quiet recently, she's not found a man for herself has she?' Maureen asked.

'Not as far as I've heard. I expect she's found another project to get her teeth into.'

'There's nothing like a good project,' Maureen said.

'Speaking of which, I need to ask you something,' Frank said, though he hadn't really planned to say anything just yet just. Keeping information from Maureen was getting tougher.

'Fire ahead,'

'I was wondering how you'd feel if I tried to find my father. I don't want to upset you, so would only do it with your blessing,' Frank said.

'I wondered when this might come up,' she replied. 'I know that's what people do these days, search for their family. I can't blame you but it won't be easy when we have such little information. I did have a half-hearted try myself in the 60s but didn't get far.'

'Not even with your librarian skills?' Frank tried to tease her but the other end of the line was unresponsive.

Eventually Maureen spoke. 'The US were cagey over releasing documents and there was no internet back then. Your grandmother was furious I'd even tried.'

'Well, I hope you won't be furious if I tell you we've already tracked down Sheila Grimshaw. There might be more she can tell us.'

'Sheila Grimshaw... well I never! Where did you find her?'

'It's a long story but she's called Sheila Bramwich now and she's a retired teacher who writes children's stories.'

'Good heavens!' Maureen managed a smile. 'I'd love to meet her again. Where does she live?'

'Ah, we haven't got that far... possibly Luton but we don't have an address yet. Apricot is exploring it through her library connections. I've asked Apricot not to say much until I've spoken to you. I imagine that's why she's been quiet.'

'At least she's not dropped me and that's why you said *we* were searching,' Maureen said, sounding happier.

'It's me, Apricot and Mirabelle,' Frank confessed. 'I couldn't do it on my own.'

'Fair enough. Anyone else looking into my private business?'

'No, Mum and if you want us to stop, we will but it would be nice for you to meet Sheila, wouldn't it? And she might remember things about the chap she got off with that night, which could lead us to Jimmy.'

'Okay, I can see where you're going with this,' she said.

'So, do we have permission to give Sheila your address so she can write to you? It won't make you too anxious, will it?'

'I don't really have much choice. Yes, go ahead.'

'Thanks, Mum. I had intended to have this conversation face-to-face but I couldn't keep you in the dark any longer.'

'You're a good man, Frank but don't let your expectations be too high. I don't want you hurt any more than you have been. I'm tired now, let's say goodnight.'

'Yes, goodnight, Mum. I'll phone tomorrow to see how you are.'

CHAPTER 49

Once she'd found Sheila's address, Apricot sent a copy of the letter to Frank for his approval. It was a charming letter, explaining who she was and why she'd made contact. She didn't mention at this stage that her friends were looking for Jimmy, just worked with the idea of Maureen wanting to get back in touch. It was, of course, just right - clear and unobtrusive.

After some back-and-forth communication, it was agreed Sheila could be given Maureen's address and they would write to each other.

It wasn't long before the two women wanted to meet face-to-face. Maureen had by then gathered that Sheila was widowed but still fit for her age. With winter approaching with darker evenings, Sheila's daughter, Ali, offered to drive her mother across from Bedfordshire. They thought they might stay in a hotel up the coast for a few days and make a short holiday of it.

'Are you sure you don't want someone with you when you first meet?' Frank asked when he phoned Maureen about the arrangements.

'I'd rather break the ice on my own. It's been so long since we met and there'll be a lot of catching up to do. It won't all be about Bungay Village Hall.'

'Bungay Community Hall!' Frank spluttered. 'Jeez, I'm stupid – only just put two and two together. It's no wonder you were desperate to come to my concert.'

'I really did want to hear you sing but I must say there was something else drawing me in.'

'Bungay-whatever-it's-called-Hall. Bloody hell!' Frank repeated. 'Why on earth didn't I cotton on sooner? Perhaps it's a good job I didn't, I'd never have been able to sing, knowing I'd been conceived there.'

'That's enough of that sort of talk. Now you can see why I want my first conversation with Sheila to be private.'

'What about Ali?'

'I might suggest she goes walkabout. We'll see.'

'And you'll phone me in the evening to tell me how it's gone?'

'I will.'

'I'll have my phone with me all day in case you need me. I can come whenever necessary.'

'Settle down, Frank. This is two old friends meeting up, not a hearing at the Old Bailey,' Maureen said. 'I've made a nice Madeira cake and Cathy's given the place a good clean. It'll be fine.'

It'll be fine.

The evening after Sheila's visit, Frank checked his phone every half hour. When it rang, he picked it up on the first buzz.

'You alright, Mum?' he asked.

'Yes, fine.'

'You sound odd,' Frank said.

'Just tired.'

'Shall I come?

'Yes, come tomorrow. There's too much to

366

say on the phone.'

'Promise you're okay, though?

'I promise. I'll tell you all about it in the morning. Come in time for lunch, and there's some cake left.'

Frank drove up as early as was acceptable to be visiting a seventy-nine-year-old woman with severe arthritis who found it hard to get going in the mornings. Despite still being at the breakfast table reading the newspaper, his mother seemed pleased to see him.

'All good then, Mum?' Frank asked, pouring himself a cup of tea and joining her.

'We had such a good time. Sheila was very chatty and Ali was delightful, in the end she stayed while we talked.'

'And did you get any useful information?'

'Well, the conversation started slowly and we did the obvious catch up stuff, you know, what we'd been up to for the past sixty odd years.'

'That must have taken a while,' Frank said, straightening his cup on its saucer.

'Ali said she wished she'd recorded it. Anyway, then we got on to what happened that night, Sheila honestly didn't know it had resulted in a baby. Her memory was poor at first but the more we talked, the more we both remembered things.'

'And what was she able to tell you?' Frank asked impatiently.

'Her father's printing company did some work for the Air Force and that was why we got invited to the dance, apparently they needed more girls. Anyway, he drove us there and arranged for a young colleague to bring us home.'

'And what was the name of Sheila's catch?' Frank asked.

'Oh, Frank, don't call him that. Her dancing partner was called Ossie, short for Oswald. Oswald Clifford Brown II was Jimmy's best friend and then when we talked about the songs we danced to that night. She came up with the fact that Jimmy's surname was Martin, like Dean Martin.'

'How come she remembered that and you didn't?' Frank said.

'She and Ossie had met up a few days after the dance. They liked each other a lot and he wanted to say goodbye properly because the lads were going back to the States the very next day. That's when they reminisced about the song that was played for their last dance.'

'Sounds rather romantic,' Frank said.

'It was a Dean Martin song and they'd laughed that he might be related to his friend Jimmy Martin.'

'Amazing,' Frank said with a smile and started humming "Memories Are Made Of This".

'How did you know?'

'It's a famous song, we've sung an arrangement of it at choir.'

'Really?! Anyway, together they decided not to tell me anything about Jimmy Martin because it turned out he had a fiancée back home.'

'Whoops! Sheila wasn't such a great friend then?' Frank said.

'It wasn't her fault. At the time I hadn't told her the full extent of what we got up to that night. She thought we just kissed a bit. She had no idea why I might need to keep in touch.'

'Did she and Ossie stay in contact?'

'No, they decided long distance relationships never worked out. They just said a fond goodbye and that was it.'

'And you and Sheila never talked about it again?' Frank queried.

'We didn't meet up again. It was the summer holidays; I was back in Eastland and Sheila's family went away on a long trip.'

Maureen started to look upset.

'Don't tell me any more Mum. You did really well finding Jimmy's name. That's enough for now.'

'No, there's something else; apparently, my mother rang Mrs Grimshaw when they returned from their travels and gave her a piece of her mind for not taking proper care of me when I was staying in her house. She blamed Sheila for not keeping an eye on me. It was your grandmother who severed all relations with the Grimshaws, not the other way round as I always thought.'

'Oh dear, I'm so sorry.'

'My own stupid mother decreed I'd never see my best friend again,' Maureen said.

She pulled a hanky from her sleeve and blew her nose.

'I suppose we can't blame, Sheila then,' Frank said.

'No, Sheila's mother never told her about the baby.'

'And it was your mother who ran the show from then on.'

'I'm afraid it was. Remember things were very different in the 50s. I must say Ali was suitably shocked by the whole story. She'd worked as a senior midwife and was very interested, at a professional level, as well as being understanding. She asked all about how a teenage pregnancy was handled in those days. I found it quite cathartic to talk about it.'

'Jimmy Martin, or maybe he calls himself James. I now know the name of my father,' Frank said thoughtfully.

CHAPTER 50

Mirabelle and Frank were able to ask for more information from the Lakenheath Archive now they had the name James 'Jimmy' Martin. Frank kept an eye on the post and checked his emails regularly for any updates, while Mirabelle searched the internet for more leads. They kept in touch, were pally on the phone and on one of their longer phone calls, Frank told Mirabelle, in confidence, what he'd learned about Tricia and Gus.

Mirabelle and Frank's friendship grew closer again and occasionally they visited each other but never stayed overnight. As Christmas approached, Frank wanted to buy Mirabelle a present to thank her for all her help. On his way to a football match with Geoff one evening, Frank spotted a poster on the wall outside. Jools Holland and his Orchestra were to play at the Ipswich Regent, with Ruby Turner in support.

'Great singer,' said Geoff. 'It's sold out but as it happens, I've got two spare tickets if you're interested. The wife and I were going to take some friends and they've had to pull out. I was planning to return them to the box office but if you want them, they're yours.'

'Let me think, I'm not working that night. Yes, I'll take them off your hands. How much do I owe you?'

The deal was completed and Felixstowe and Walton FC won their match against Canvey Island. Once home after a great evening, all

Frank had to do was phone Mirabelle and check she was free.

Walking to the Regent, Frank and Mirabelle talked about their plans for the festive season.

'I'm spending Christmas Eve and Christmas Day with Mum then I'll bring her back to Felixstowe to stay with me for a day or two so at last she can see my flat.'

'That sound lovely,' Mirabelle said. 'I'm so pleased for you, Frank, having Christmas with your mum.'

'I've booked the whole week off work. It'll be a real first,' Frank said. 'I was wondering...'

'Don't tell me, you want me to make you a Christmas pudding for the occasion?' Mirabelle interrupted.

'Actually, I wondered if you'd like to join us on Boxing Day?'

'That's sweet of you but I thought I'd told you I was spending Christmas week in Wales with Andy. We'll probably have Christmas Day with the Jones family at a local hotel. It'll be our first family Christmas for ages too.'

'Christmas with Les? You must be mad,' Frank exploded.

'We've been divorced for years, so it's no big deal and I'd like to see my ex-mother-in-law again. Andy's partner's been invited too and Les' new fiancée might put in an appearance. It'll be truly fascinating.'

'You're a brave woman, Mirabelle Jones.'

'We've talked it through on the phone and it'll be very civilised. Christmas Day itself could

'I'm from Manchester,' James said, 'Mancunian through and through.'

'City or United?' Frank asked. Mirabelle kicked him and frowned.

'United, of course,' James replied.

'Congratulations on the engagement,' Mirabelle said, quickly changing the subject. 'Did you know about the engagement, Celine or was it a lovely surprise?'

'I had an inkling. They're just down from Manchester for the birthday weekend but I sensed something else was going on. At least it's good news for a change,' she added.

Frank got himself together, realising that polite conversation was in order, but maybe not football talk. He tried not to stare at what looked like a new scar with visible black stitches, that was hiding behind a faded ringlet on the side of Tricia's forehead. He asked if Celine's wife was with them and although distracted, he heard someone say Lynn had a migraine and they thought the loud music and flashing lights wouldn't be wise.

'Guess not,' Frank said. 'I hope she soon feels better. It's very nice to put a face to the name, Celine. I know how fond of you my Aunt Della is. And Tricia, it's nice to see you looking happy and I trust, well.' His eyes flicked momentarily back to the scar.

'I'm surprised you recognised me. Don't mind this little thing,' Tricia giggled as she flicked back the curl. 'I've had a small skin cancer removed and I've not been able to dye my hair recently so I've decided to go natural.'

'And no more sun-beds for you either, my darling,' James added. 'You are beautiful as you are.'

Frank nudged Mirabelle and said they should return to their friends.

'Yes, we must go back to our seats too. Good to meet you both,' Celine said.

'Might see you on the way out. Enjoy the second half,' Mirabelle said.

'That was fun, but what was the football question about?' she asked, when they were back in their seats.

'Just trying to be friendly to James. Did it sound a bit random?' Frank asked.

'Just a bit. Never mind. And you really shouldn't have drawn attention to the scar. A more sensitive woman would have been mortified.'

'As you might gather, Tricia is not a particularly sensitive woman,' Frank replied.

'No, I can see that. She seemed quite pleasant, and astonishingly open about her recent operation,' Mirabelle said. 'Let's hope they removed all the cancer cells. I must say I wouldn't be smiling about it.'

'Her mind might not work like other people's,' Frank commented.

'Or maybe it's given her a fright and that, alongside turning forty, is making her re-evaluate her life.'

'One of your most endearing features, dear Mirabelle, is how you see the best in everyone,' Frank said as they settled in their seats.

'I wonder where they're sitting. Oh look, way over there.' Mirabelle looked as if she was going to wave so Frank grabbed her hand.

'Leave it, love. I think we've seen enough of them. James Martin! Would you fathom it.'

'He seemed nice, too. I think she's in good hands there,' Mirabelle said.

It seemed to Frank that she was giving him permission to stop thinking about Tricia. 'I think we've done enough mingling. When this is over, we'll leave discretely through the side door.'

'You're being very decisive this evening, Frank. I like it. We need to go out more.'

Mirabelle jiggled, tapped her feet and swayed when the music started up again. After the encore and some exhausting clapping, they slipped away and walked slowly back to Mirabelle's place, chatting about the songs they liked best. At the door, Mirabelle stopped.

'It's quite late, Frank. Why don't you stay?'

'Are you sure?'

'Sure,' she said.

CHAPTER 51

Frank worked full time in the lead up to Christmas but phoned Mirabelle daily. There seemed to be no more news about Jimmy Martin, but Frank didn't know how hard Mirabelle was working in the background to actually find the man in America.

He and Mirabelle both admitted they were sad to not now be spending the holidays together. On the morning of Christmas Eve, they wished each other safe journeys and promised to phone again the next day. Frank drove to Lowestoft and found Cathy had helped Maureen put lights round the front door and decorated the house. The mantelpiece was laden with cards and there was a small pile of presents under the tree.

'This all looks lovely. It's a far cry from Christmas at Mrs West's. I always used to offer to work on Christmas Day in the past.'

'I used to go down to Reg and Della's but couldn't make it the last few years. This is a real treat for me too,' Maureen said.

'And you look so well, I do hope you enjoy it.'

'I plan to. I hope you'll come to church with me in the morning. I like to go if I can on special days. I'm told the Brownies helped decorate the Christmas tree in church this year.'

'Sure, I'll come. I'll enjoy a good sing.'

'Cathy will be there with her family too. We'll go to the ten o'clock service, then come back to open our presents before lunch.' She looked at the bag of gifts Frank had brought. 'Pop yours under the tree.'

Christmas Day went to plan and by the evening, Maureen was dozing in her chair. Frank went to his room to call Mirabelle - they'd only exchanged the briefest "Happy Christmas" call that morning.

'How did lunch go?'

'It was fine,' she said.

'You've been drinking, haven't you?' he laughed.

'I needed something to get through it. No, it's been okay actually, nice food and the new fiancée was quite pleasant, pretty but a bit dull. They're welcome to each other.'

'And Andy behaved?'

'Not bad at all, considering the booze was flowing. It was good to see him with his father and of course, Mrs Jones Senior was thrilled to see everyone. She's ancient now, and deaf, so we didn't really speak much. She grinned at me a lot so I took that as a pass.'

'Well, I'm glad there were no soap opera scenes. We've been quiet but it's been a nice day. Mum's all packed for the journey to Felixstowe tomorrow. We'll go in the afternoon once we've cleared up here.'

'And your fridge and freezer are well stocked up?'

'All organised. Have you heard from Apricot? She sent Mum a lovely card and a box of chocolate truffles. Real cream, so we're taking them back with us to eat while they're still in date.'

'Apricot will be exhausted after working all day at the Crisis Centre. I'll call her tomorrow.'

'She's amazing, isn't she? Always helping other people.'

'You sound as if you've been drinking now, Frank,' Mirabelle chuckled.

'I promise I haven't,' he replied.

'I know. Only teasing.'

'Must tell you something. Mum and I have been asked to go to lunch at Della's on New Year's Day. When are you travelling back?'

'Why, am I invited?' Mirabelle asked.

'Not sure but we did say we'd to do something together this New Year?'

'It doesn't have to be New Year's Day itself but I will be back by then. I've booked a train for the 30th,' Mirabelle said.

'I'm running Mum back home just after New Year, probably the 2nd. You could come with us. I'll not be staying over. We can just settle her in and then return home.'

'Yes, let's do that,' Mirabelle answered. 'Families are lovely but they can make planning dates more complicated.'

'Good though, isn't it? I'm hoping we have the whole year to make dates,' Frank said. 'Oh, and thanks for the diary and the jumper.'

'Pleasure. Hope it fits. And thank you for the perfume - my favourite. I bet Apricot gave you some advice,' Mirabelle said.

'Of course.'

'Better go now. Andy's planning a game of charades and as you might imagine, I am an expert.'

'I hate charades. We'll be watching a film. Happy rest of Christmas, Mirabelle.'

'Happy Christmas, Frank.'

Della's plans for a New Year's Day lunch expanded. She added name after name to her list and then worried it would be too much of a crowd for her bungalow. She counted them repeatedly, knowing even eight people at her table would be tight. Gus and Sandra would be there, as well as Frank and Maureen. Frank had then asked if Mirabelle could come, and Della, in the spirit of Christmas, agreed. Celine was being a helper as well as a guest, so Lynn had to be fitted in too. Della insisted Alfie the dog would have to stay at home. That made eight for the meal but then she'd mentioned it to Oliver and Charlotte and suggested they arrive later with the twins for desserts. She then thought it would be a great opportunity to have Jenny, Max and the children over too.

'You can't manage all that, Della. I know you're feeling much better but it's madness,' Sandra said when she heard the plan. 'It'll be too much with all the children too.'

'Of course I can manage. It's children who make Christmas special and I haven't seen anything of them during the festive season. Oliver's lot have been at Charlotte's mother and the Browns have been at Jenny's parents.'

'I've had a thought; our house isn't much bigger than yours but The Treehouse Café will be closed to the public. Why not have a meal there and we can make a party of it?'

'I don't want you to have to do anything dear, you've not got long to go 'til the baby now. It's you who should be resting.'

'I'm fine, Della. Baby girl's looking good on her recent scan and I still have a few weeks. Celine will be there to help and I might even ask the chef from the restaurant what he can do for us. I'll call him.'

'It's a girl! Oh, Sandra that's wonderful,' Della said.

'Shhh, no one else knows apart from Gus,' Sandra grinned.

Chef did them a fabulous three course meal. Maureen sat next to Della and the two talked happily. Maureen just had one glass of wine, no doubt to be sociable but Della had none. She was watching over her guests and saw Gus was keeping a close eye on Sandra, ordering her to sit down all the time, while Celine and Lynn fussed round everyone else and helped serve. Frank and Mirabelle looked quite at home as conversation flowed around the table. There was a pause between the main course and desserts and Della saw Gus and Frank go outside for a walk. She hoped they wouldn't lock horns again. Things had settled down so well between them since last January and as for her, there was nothing like a serious illness and having a granddaughter on the way, to get life in perspective.

Della nudged Maureen. "Do you think the boys will be all right? Should someone check up on them?'

'No. They're grown-ups now. I think they've found the good bits in each other and are even starting to like the idea of being cousins,' Maureen said.

'I'm sad Reg made such a mess of his will, it was nearly the end of us as a family,' Della said. 'Some of it was probably my fault.'

'Not entirely, I know he could be on the strange side, not always easy. He took after our mother.'

'Old Mrs Hall,' Della said and they both sniggered.

'Anyway, that's all in the past now,' said Maureen. 'You have hope for the future and so do I.'

'Yes, and your Frank's turned out better than expected.'

'He's a decent man and I think Mirabelle's been good for him. She whispered to me earlier that she's still been looking for his father, even though Frank has stepped back a bit from the idea. She's found a new lead in South Carolina and she wanted my permission to tell Frank.'

'Good of her to check with you but if you're not happy about it you must tell her,' Della said.

'I'm pleased for him. I don't want any personal contact, it's too late for that, but if she's really found his dad, Frank deserves to know. She wants to tell him this evening when he takes her home.'

'That sound good. I'm sorry I've never acknowledged the difficulties you had to deal with in your life. I know I've been harsh at times and slow to welcome Frank into the family,' Della said.

'You've had tough times too, my dear,' Maureen said.

'Look out, here comes trouble.'

Della stood up and opened her arms. Jacob and Mabel ran to hug her, followed by Issy and Willow. Jenny and Charlotte came in next, arm in arm and smiling, with Oliver, Gus and Max not far behind. Frank came through the door last and went to stand behind Mirabelle's chair. Della noticed Jacob was grinning happily at Frank, who leaned forward and put his hands on Mirabelle's shoulders as if marking his territory. Della glanced across and nodded to her sister-in-law.

CHAPTER 53

Frank drove Mirabelle home to Ipswich that afternoon, deciding he'd return to fetch his mother later and give Maureen one more night in his flat before taking her home to Lowestoft. He hummed along with the tunes on the radio as he drove.

'That was a lovely day, Frank, thank you for including me. Have you time for a cup of tea before you go back for your mum?' Mirabelle asked.

'I think I can manage it,' Frank said. 'Mum's popping over to Della's and will wait for me there.'

Mirabelle's house was warm and cosy. The front room had been tidied and there was a new painting on the easel, waiting to be finished. Frank liked this house very much but he also liked his new home. There really was no reason they couldn't enjoy both, each have their own space but still be a couple.

Frank turned to Mirabelle. 'I think we are good together but we each like our own places. How about being a couple with two homes for the time being?'

'That could work,' Mirabelle smiled.

'Now we can afford it, I think that might be the answer, Mirabelle.'

'The answer to us you mean?'

'Yes, us. Also, I've been thinking about my dad in America, I'd like to go and look for him this coming year. Would you come with me?'

'Oh, Frank!' she said, taking a deep breath.

Frank's heart sank, ready for a refusal. Was it too much to ask, had he got his timing wrong and messed up again?

'I've been wanting to tell you something but I had to check with Maureen first.'

'Oh, God, what is it?'

'I think I might have located James "Jimmy" Martin in South Carolina.'

'Are you serious?' Frank asked.

'Deadly serious. I was planning to tell you all the details this evening when we had a moment to ourselves. Your mum's happy for you to try and find him. I think your plan to go to America is just the thing,' Mirabelle grinned like Ricky the Cheshire cat. 'And seeing as you've asked so nicely, I'd love to come with you.'

They kissed warmly, happily, giggling like youngsters.

'This is the best New Year I've ever had,' Frank said when he stopped to draw breath.

'Get your diary out, Frank, and we'll look at some dates. 2020 is going to be quite a year.'

Acknowledgements

I am so grateful to everybody who has helped me with this book, in particular my friends at Wivenhoe Writers Group and the Shed Writers. Special thanks go to Sue Dawes, who undertook an early edit and analysis of the manuscript. She continues to keep an eye on my writing, as does Helen Chambers.

Thank you to my husband for his long-suffering support and to two more early readers, Sarah Harwood and Jeanne Hale. Every ounce of encouragement has been truly valued.

I wish to thank Blossom Spring Publishing for taking on 'To Be Frank' and look forward to many readers enjoying this book.

About The Author

Philippa Hawley is a writer living in NE Essex with her husband and several tortoises. They have two grown-up children, and a busy, toddler grandchild who visits often. Having worked as a family doctor in the NHS for over 30 years Philippa has been privileged to observe human behaviour and relationships in close proximity, and this comes across in her writing which often includes medical topics presented in a subtle and accessible way.

Philippa is an active member of local writing groups with whom she shares short stories, flash fiction and sometimes poetry. Philippa enjoys travel writing when travel is possible, and she has also self-published three contemporary fiction novels since 2013, making 'To Be Frank' her fourth novel.

When not writing, Philippa likes watching films and reading. She also spends time in her garden maintaining a wildlife area which backs onto the local woods, attracting wonderful birds, butterflies and dragonflies.

Philippa Hawley
www.philippahawley.com
@philippa_hawley

www.blossomspringpublishing.com

Printed in Great Britain
by Amazon

81526981R00226